THE HOPPERNOTS

THE HOPPERNOTS

DEBORAH BLAKE DEMPSEY

Cover Art by Jet Kimchrea

Summary: When Max, Cristobel, and Spyder discover legendary creatures they believed were the figment of the Elders imagination, they vow to discover why they have returned. Catching the evil creatures destroying their home and attacking an Elder, the trio must make everyone forget their troublemaking past and trust them to lead them in a fight for the lake they call home or risk losing it…and their lives.

Library of Congress Control Number: 2014911037

ISBN
978-0-9904812-0-1 (paperback)
978-0-9904812-1-8 (eBook)

[1. Frogs–Fiction. 2. Adventure and adventurers–Fiction. 3. Fantasy–Fiction. 4. Friendship–Fiction. 5. Human-animal relationships.–Fiction. 5. Humorous stories. 6. Animals–Fiction. 7. Amphibians–Fiction.]

Published by
PUG PAW PRESS
P.O. Box 896
Londonderry, NH 03053

This book was typeset in Big Caslon.

Lovingly dedicated to

Shelley Molina Maas

Cooper (the best pug in the world) Dempsey

Ashling Chantal Bagnall

table of Contents

one
Luna Light Night

It was the beginning of the evening festivities on Lake Fibian. The last of winter's chilly fingers loosened their grip, as early spring transformed the earth from barren and leafless to budding and lush.

All around the lake clusters of frogs gathered at the edge of the murky green water. Above them night-dewed trees rustled and swayed. The warm evening breeze swirled the scents of the lake through the air – the damp smell of the earth, old fallen leaves and the lingering salty-sweet scent of late afternoon rain. Through the trees and dancing above the glistening water, lightning bugs buzzed around the crowd, casting shimmer and light on the water.

Some frogs found their favorite spots and remained rooted while others pushed and slipped into tight-knotted groups. The rest found any place they could cling to or burrow under, leaving only their curious eyes above ground.

The noise level grew and the earth sounded like a symphony tuning up.

Nearing the large trunk of an oak tree, three young frogs rushed to join the crowd.

"Hurry! Hurry! We're late." Cristobel yelled back to her two friends hopping behind her.

"But, we're almoth there," Spyder said. His large blue belly heaved rapidly. "Do we have to leap the whole way, Crithobel?"

"The beginning is the best part," Max chirped. He hopped past them, a wide grin spread across his green face.

"I think the food is the best part," Spyder grumbled, which reminded him of the feast to come. He sped up.

"I can't wait to get to the lake," Cristobel squealed. She sprang forward and caught up to Max. They entered the clearing and arrived at the mouth of Lake Fibian.

Cristobel and Max stopped and leaned against a squat purple mushroom to catch their breath while they waited for Spyder to catch up.

When Spyder arrived, huffing and puffing, they hopped forward and looked for a spot close to the water's edge. Their laughter joined the cacophony of frog voices as they watched the band, The Spadefoots, tune their instruments.

Cristobel hopped up and down, then chirped. "Can you feel it?"

"Feel what?" Max asked.

"You can feel my belly gwumbling, can't you?" Spyder asked. His belly was demanding, always rumbling with its need for food.

"Not your stomach, silly." Cristobel raised a hand and rubbed her flat fingers against her ear. "Something exciting is going to happen tonight. I can feel it."

"Maybe there will be new appetizers," Spyder said. "I'd love some worm puffs or snails wrapped in crispy beetle legs."

Cristobel puffed out her cheeks and continued to hop in place. Max gazed around and noted a few missing frogs.

"I wish one of us lived closer to the lake." Max grumbled. "We could have stayed home and watched from the windows."

Max looked over at a nearby tree and saw frogs from different species clinging to rough bark like autumn leaves. He sighed when he saw mushroom-topped roofs and tall twig condos covered with squirming excited bodies.

Chirping in revelry a rushing group of Spring Peepers pushed Cristobel aside.

"Hey, watch out!" Cristobel cried. She bumped into Spyder's stomach, bounced off his round belly and landed on her bottom. Max and Spyder laughed and helped her up.

The boys stood on either side of Cristobel. She looped her arms through theirs, linking them together. It was harder to get knocked down this way.

Once a month, on Luna Light Night the Anura — the entire frog nation —gathered around Lake Fibian to celebrate the unity of the lake. The bright, circular orb suspended high in the air, lit the lake, and lured frogs from every tree, burrow, or lily pad together to swap stories, share a laugh or sometimes to discuss problems or concerns, but mostly, it was to celebrate.

Cristobel looked out over the water, then at her two friends. "It's hard to believe we wouldn't be friends if the Anura still fought each other."

Lake Fibian's history, to the shock and delight of the leaplings, was a mixture of battles, secrets, and misdeeds. It wasn't only the frogs who fought. All the animal species that lived at the lake fought each other, but the worst battles were between the different species of the Anura.

Cristobel, Max, and Spyder, affectionately known by all the animals of Lake Fibian as *The Three*, were from different, and previously warring, species. If the battles existed, they would not be friends today.

Among the Anura, the trio were an odd sight to see. While the other species of the Anura got along well enough, they tended to have friendships within their own species, but seeing *The Three's* strong bond, many of the other frogs were encouraged to look past colors, spots, stripes, and croaks.

Cristobel gazed fondly at her two friends. "Who would have thought members of the Red-Eyed Tree frogs, the Strawberry Poison-Darts, and the Polka Dot Tree frogs could be friends like we are."

"And we are the vewy best of friends," Spyder said.

"We have an unbreakable friendship," Max added.

Max hailed from the Red-Eyed Tree frog species. He blended in with lakeside flora, which was good...when he was up to no good. Seen from above, his head and back were bright green. Seen from below, his golden belly usually quivered with laughter. His strong arms and legs were blue and his webbed hands and feet were bright orange. His eyes were a delightful shade of red that usually held a twinkle.

Being an only sib-leapling, Max thought of Spyder as his brother-frog and couldn't imagine them not being friends. They met as tadpoles and had seen each other every day since they lost their tails.

Spyder was a Strawberry Poison Dart frog. His real name was Bates, but Max nicknamed him Spyder because his head, upper back and arms were bright red and his lower body and feet were brilliant blue with thin black lines that ran around his body like a spider's web.

They became fast friends when Max stood up for Spyder when other tadpoles made fun of his tangled tongue. Spyder also had a speech snag that twisted his words, but made listening to him fun.

Cristobel was a Polka-Dot Tree frog. Max and Spyder didn't like girl frogs very much since most were squeamish and giggly, but they thought Cristobel was cool for a girl frog. Her skin was bright yellow with gentle shades of green and red. Her expressive white eyes and air of innocence usually got them out of trouble.

To the Lake Fibian community *The Three* were a wonderful sight. The trio was usually seen bounding and leaping by with their bright colors and constant laughter. They reminded everyone, and not only the

Anura, of the importance of keeping the peace and working together.

On this particular evening, the air was electric. A strange hum tinged the oncoming night. Every frog felt the buzz in the air like industrious bees making honey.

The Spadefoots finished tuning up their wooden, leaf, and stone-made instruments and were ready to play the Lake Fibian anthem. Rows and rows of frogs prepared their throats, expanding and contracting their fleshy underbellies in preparation to sing the opening song of Luna Light Night.

Mister Webster, one of the oldest and a well-respected member of the Anura, was the conductor of The Spadefoots. He lifted his long arms and tapped two thin reeds together getting everyone's attention. They settled down and prepared to sing.

DEBORAH BLAKE DEMPSEY

Many years ago
On the Lake of Fibian
Lake Fibian . . .

Frog upon frog
Would not give in
Lake Fibian . . .

To the beauty of our kinship
Or the comfort of a friend
Lake Fibian . . .

Where frog against frog
Fought to the bitter end
Lake Fibian . . .

We were grouped against each other
With problems all around
Lake Fibian . . .

But we found a way to listen and
Turned our problems upside-down
Lake Fibian . . .

Now we help when it is needed
We give counsel when we can
Lake Fibian . . .

We grow and work together
For a positive Anura end
Lake Fibian . . .

We love like a family
We are very good friends
Lake Fibian . . .

Now that we all live
Happily, on . . .
Lake Fibian

After the last note was played, loud applause—*chirps, snorts, croaks* and *cracks*—rippled around the lake. The moon's beams shined so bright, the colors of each frog species looked like flashing jewels.

Max chirped and looked around. After all the stories he'd heard about the battles that happened long before he'd hatched, he was filled with happiness because everyone got along.

Every frog was told Croaklores in the early tadpole years. Tales of when Lake Fibian was a dangerous place. A time when a fabled creature called the Hoppernot lived amongst them and frogs did not trust each other, unless they came from the same species. Max's grandfather used to tell him stories of the great battles that took place like the War of the Water Way, the Lily Pad Revolt and of his own near misses with the Hoppernot.

Half of him believed the tales, but the other half could not imagine he and his friends—the frog and the other animal species—could be mortal enemies.

The band played another tune.

"It's the Frog Salsa," Cristobel yelled. She grabbed Max's arms and swung him around in a hopping, bouncing, leaping motion. Max laughed, then wheezed when she picked up speed and twirled him. The lake and the other dancers became a blur.

While the band played and the frogs danced and talked, the Luna Light Night caterers slipped between frogs handing out seaweed poppers and cricket-in-a-blanket appetizers to the hungry crowd.

Spyder hopped up and down to see if a server was near.

"I hope it's a fwoggy we know. Maybe I can talk them into giving us a whole platter full of cwicket-in-a-blanket. I'm so vewy hungwy," he said, rubbing his belly.

"I don't know how you can eat so much," Cristobel mused. "You always have a fly-pop or earthworm water taffy with you. Don't you ever get tired of eating, Spy?"

Instead of answering, Spyder darted over to a Luna Light Night waiter who also happened to be his cousin Harold. Cristobel and Max watched as Harold looked around, and then shoved a tray into Spyder's hands and dived back into the crowd, distancing himself from his always hungry cousin.

"I got it." He wiggled his body and laughed. "That's my favowite cousin of all time," Spyder said, through a mouth full of crunchy crickets. He held the tray out to his friends.

"I thought thing-a-ma-frog was your favorite cousin," Max said. He picked up a fat wiggly blanket, threw it high in the air and darted his tongue out to catch it.

"Oh Max, haven't you figured it out yet?" Cristobel asked, giggling as she turned to him. "His favorite cousin is always the last cousin who put food in his hands."

"It's twue. My stomach is a family curse. We all love to eat-eat-eat."

"I'm amazed you haven't blown up yet." Max laughed and stuffed his mouth with as many seaweed poppers his cheeks could hold.

"Not yet, but I did hear about a gweat-gweat-gweat-gweat-gweat-gweat uncle—" he stopped to count on his sticky fingers, "—who exploded after he ate a bunch of slug sandwiches." Spyder beamed after that bit of news.

"Crithobel, are you going to eat any more?"

"How many is a bunch? Nine? Ten?" Max asked.

"About twenty-six . . . or was it thirty-two," Spyder pondered. He scratched the side of his nostril. "I can't wemember, but he's a legend in the family."

"The only legend in my family was my cousin Tessera," Cristobel said.

"What'd she do?" Max asked, his mouth full of crunchy crickets. He swallowed and burped his appreciation.

Cristobel grabbed a handful of seaweed poppers before they disappeared. She tossed a couple into her mouth before she answered.

"Cousin Tessera was the only member of my family to leave Lake Fibian." She chewed slowly as she thought. "She was one of the few Anura who ever left. When she came back, she told my aunt and the Elders crazy stories about frogs with two heads, six legs, missing eyes and water that burns when you jump into it. Of course, they didn't believe her. They tried to get her to see Doctor Tom, but she insisted she was telling the truth. When no one believed her, she left. No one has seen her since."

Max and Spyder's mouths hung open. Spyder didn't even attempt to snatch the low flying mosquito out of the air.

"Was your cousin Madcap Tess?" Max asked, awed by the news. Madcap Tess was a frog who, it was said, lost her froggy mind.

"That's her," she said.

Max asked, "Why didn't you tell us?"

"We don't talk about her. It upsets my aunt. Anyway, I never knew her. She left long before I was hatched. She's probably dead by now and . . . hey, watch out."

Cristobel hopped to the side as she was almost knocked over, this time by two reveling Hourglass Tree

Frogs, with overflowing cups of Chipmunk Delight—a special brew made from wild plums, worms, fly legs, and blueberries—bounced by. "Anyway, I doubt she had half the adventures we've had."

"That's twue," Spyder said. "We've had some goo—" he burped, "—good times."

Max's tongue lolled out of his mouth while he thought about this. They had some cool adventures under their sweetgrass belts, most of which no one but the three of them knew about. Like climbing to the top of Archibald the Redwood tree, and escaping BlooBlaq, the grumpy Black Vulture every amphibian and rodent was careful to avoid.

"I still can't believe we tried to go to Barrier Lake," Cristobel whispered.

"I can't believe we didn't get caught," Max replied.

Barrier Lake was a forbidden place where the rules of living didn't exist. Since most of the Elders were distracted with preparing for the first Luna Light Night of the season, the trio snuck off just that morning. A hundred leaps before arriving there they almost lost their lives when they jumped into the snake pit of the notorious Limmon and his snake den. It was early spring. Who knew they'd be there already?

Luckily, Limmon and the rest of the snake nest were still too groggy from the Deep Sleep, so Max,

Spyder, and Cristobel escaped before they became snake food.

"We get too caught up in the fun and this time we almost learned the hard way to pay attention to our surroundings," Cristobel said.

The protection under the Lake Fibian Collaboration Agreement did not extend as far as Barrier Lake.

"The predator species over there are not obligated to *not* to attack other animals," Cristobel added.

"Close call, that one," Max said.

"I guess Madcap Tess isn't vewy big news after Blooblaq and Bawwier Lake," Spyder said. He sighed and licked his hand.

"I think it's just another Croaklore to keep us in line," Cristobel said. "I doubt Cousin Tessera left the lake. I bet she hid out for a while to get away from . . ."

Cristobel didn't have a chance to finish as Max laid his hand on her arm and croaked, "Listen."

In silence, Cristobel, Max, and Spyder listened to the odd grunting sounds coming from behind them. They turned their bodies around to face the direction of the noise and watched as frogs swayed and fell as if a heavy wind blew.

What they saw was not a natural force knocking frogs over, but two very real and very frightened Anura Elders.

two
The Sighting

"May I have your attention, please?" Mister Wally Fowler's voice quivered. Most of the crowd, still excited by Luna Light Night, did not hear the Mayor's trembling voice. The Spadefoots continued to play. The music grew louder as the voices of the crowd intensified.

"Please, may I have your attention?" he asked again, this time louder, but still unheard by the majority of the frogs.

"Let me try," said Titus, a brown and black bullfrog whose voice could travel across the entire lake, and whose color changed from black to brown depending on his mood. As Chief of Security, Titus knew exactly what to say to get everyone's notice. "Attention! We need the attention of the entire Anura to discuss a dire concern."

Dire. That one word stopped all conversation.

The Spadefoots, noticing Mister Webster no longer paid attention to them, paused in the middle of their song.

"Dire?" Miss Milly repeated.

Miss Milly, known around the lake as a nervous Elder frog, enjoyed fainting at the smallest thing. "Dire?" she bellowed louder, caught her breath, and then crumbled to the ground like a fallen leaf.

"Someone pick her up and lay her on the nearest lily pad please," Titus bellowed. The frogs closest to her leapt to her side and hoisted her onto their backs. As one, they hopped to the edge of the lake and laid her down on a lily pad. Cristobel hopped over with a handful of moss to place under her head.

Max realized something monumental was about to happen. He leaped over the heads of two curious frogs and landed next to Cristobel who was closer to Mister Fowler and Titus. Spyder reluctantly crept closer to his friends. His eyes darted around as he looked for an easy escape route.

"I have distressing news to tell you." Mister Fowler addressed the group. He wrung his quivering hands together. "There's been some strange activity happening at Sprocket Point House."

"Stranger than normal?" asked a chuckling voice in the crowd.

Sprocket Point House was the summer vacation spot used by most of the animals living around the lake. In summer, the house was loud and crowded with frogs and birds, lizards and squirrels, turtles and ducks and all the other types of animals of Lake Fibian. On hot summer days, they clamored to find a prime spot to relax, have fun, and stay cool.

"This is no time for jokes," Titus bellowed. "There are creatures there I have not seen for many years."

He looked around to make sure he had everyone's attention. "Not since the *Hoppernot* left."

Frightened gasps and whispers circled the lake.

The Hoppernot.

The legendary two-legged creature that had lived in Sprocket Point House, the old abandoned house up the hill from the lake's edge.

The Hoppernot used to walk around the lake upright as if sticks were stuck to its legs. It grabbed and terrorized frogs who did not move fast enough to escape its quick grasp. The Hoppernot was usually seen poking and prodding frogs and then muttering to itself in its harsh guttural language of grunts and sighs, none of the animals could understand.

Sometimes the Hoppernot entered the water and carried a long stick with a dangling string from its tip that would mesmerize the fish. In this trance-like state it was almost impossible for the fish to escape the Hoppernot's lure.

The animals became even more frightened on the few occasions the duck and pheasant flying species lost another member of their flock. Sad and nervous eyes watched the Hoppernot walk back to the house with their avian friend dangling lifeless from its hand.

That was years ago, before many of the frogs gathered now were hatched. Lake Fibian was safe now.

The Hoppernot was gone.

The last time the Hoppernot was seen, it entered a floating vessel that looked like a hollowed out, misshapen tree trunk. Scared eyes watched as it glided up the lake coast and disappeared. Never to return.

The Hoppernot appeared to have abandoned the house, and after many years of absence, Sprocket Point

House was turned into a popular vacation spot for the animals.

The presence and constant threat of the Hoppernot forced the warring Anura to agree to unify as a species. Banded together, they could defend themselves.

While the Anura agreed to harmony amongst them, the leaders from the other animal nations approached the governing frogs and asked them to join in the newly created Lake Fibian Collaboration.

The highest-ranking members of each species would be a part of the council that made up the Collaboration. Every species would have a say in running and protecting Lake Fibian.

Joining different, and sometimes unfriendly, species together was a radical idea, but the Hoppernot's presence and its preying on the animals of the lake forced them to find a way to protect themselves.

Many of the animals were opposed to the idea—the Blue Poison Dart frogs, those persnickety pests, were the loudest frogs who argued against banding together, but the stories and pleas from family members of the missing bird and fish clans, and the few frogs who lost their croak, convinced everyone.

Everyone feared the Hoppernot's return and never wanted to be vulnerable again. To seal the unity deal the Concord Pact—warning calls using notes and distinct sounds each animal species could mimic—were created to alert each other to danger.

Once the Collaboration leaders agreed to a truce between species, they decreed Lake Fibian a neutral territory. To prevent issues with the more aggressive predatory animals in the area, they declared all hunting, stalking, and feeding to be done at any of the other surrounding woods and lakes.

Mister Fowler took a deep breath. The skin beneath his chin drew in tight.

"Earlier today, we saw f-f-four Hoppernots at Sprocket Point House," he swallowed the lump in his throat.

"They appeared to be looking for something," Mister Fowler told the gathering. The growing crowd heard the fear and confusion in his voice.

"What were they looking for?" Cristobel asked.

"I don't know. They were speaking in a funny language. I couldn't understand them, but they didn't look happy. They kept shaking their heads like wet mice, but slower and moving their shoulders up and down like this." Mister Fowler demonstrated by pushing his body up and down as if he were doing push-ups.

"What did they look like?" Max asked.

"Where are they now?" Miss Milly croaked. She looked around to the frogs closest to her. Like theirs, her eyes widened with anxiety.

"Are the Hoppernots declaring war?" Cristobel asked.

Spyder raised his hand. "Is that why it brought more Hoppewnots?"

Max turned to Titus and repeated his question. "What did they look like?"

Mister Fowler looked bewildered as more and more frogs asked questions. He kept swallowing, trying to form words, but nothing squeezed past the tightness in his throat.

Noticing Mister Fowler's difficulty, Titus cut in. "I didn't see the Hoppernots myself, but I did hear strange noises behind Sprocket Point House. I went to investigate, but the Hoppernots were gone," he said. Titus paused as something niggled at the back of his mind. "You know, the area around the house looked odd, but I can't put my finger on what was different."

"We wanted to get here as soon as we could to warn you since the entire Anura are gathered," Mister Fowler added.

"Do you think they will return?" Cristobel asked. She glanced over at Max and saw his enthusiasm deflate a little.

"I don't know, but we must be careful. Pay attention no matter where you are or how safe you feel. We do not want any frogs to go missing. We'll need everyone's help watching out for these creatures in case they return," Mister Fowler said, his voice squeaked at the end.

"Of course they'll return," Miss Milly said, with a thump of her green hopping shoot. "That *thing* was always going to return."

"We never thought there would be more than one Hoppernot though," Mister Fowler said. "We should have known more of those creatures existed."

"I knew," Miss Milly sniffed. "I always said we were too complacent."

Her words brought no comfort to the crowd, who stepped closer together and glanced around as if a Hoppernot would appear at any moment. Titus glared down at her and Miss Milly promptly fainted.

In one powerful leap, Mister Fowler soared through the air and landed on a large elephant ear leaf. As he swayed, he clapped his hands together and announced, "I need everyone's attention. It is time to tell the Hoppernot Croaklore. This may be the most important telling of this Croaklore you have ever heard. So listen carefully."

A stern expression settled on Mister Fowler's wide face when a slight groan pierced the air. His mouth tightened as he watched the frogs and leaplings squirm with impatience as if the threat of Hoppernots wasn't real.

Glancing up through tree limbs to the full moon, he sighed.

After the Deep Sleep—the long hibernation during the cold winter months—the start of spring was challenging. Everyone was excited to come together again but they took for granted they were safe because the Hoppernot had been missing for so many spring cycles. That is why the telling and re-telling of the Hoppernot Croaklore was important.

Taking a deep breath, Mister Fowler began as he always began.

"The Hoppernot Croaklore is the most important lore of all the Croaklores," he bellowed.

He went silent after this announcement, letting his words sink into the minds of the frogs and leaplings gathered around him. Mister Fowler stood still, his body wide and squat, on the elephant ear leaf bouncing gently from the slight wind. He waited until most of the Anura quieted down, then pushed himself up taller and sat back on his hind legs. He folded his thin dark green hands together and scowled at three little leaplings when he heard whispers.

"Here we go again," Max muttered.

"Shh, you'll get us in trouble," Cristobel whispered.

Spyder opened his mouth to say "again" but Mister Fowler's stern expression made him snap his mouth shut.

As his eyes swept across the rest of the crowd, Mister Fowler took a few extra seconds to glare down at the three little leaplings, who continued to whisper.

Feeling the Elder frog's glare, Max pushed himself lower to the ground and out of Mister Fowler's line of sight.

"If you remember only one of these Croaklores," Mister Fowler continued, "*this* is the one you must commit to memory and heed. It may save your life."

Every year, Mister Fowler performed this lecture on the first Luna Light Night. It was one of his most important duties as Mayor of Lake Fibian, but tonight his recitation of the Hoppernot Croaklore was the most significant moment in his life.

Filling his lungs with the earth-scented air he warned, "The Hoppernot is a fiendish beast that preys on the small and defenseless. It lives on the land, but can survive in water."

Hearing a whisper, Mister Fowler darted his gaze to Cristobel, Max, and Spyder. Their innocent unblinking eyes stared back at him.

Mister Fowler cleared his throat. "The Hoppernot can climb trees as easy as a squirrel. It does not fly, but it knows the secrets of the wind. The Hoppernot can swim, and when it does, fish—and even frogs—disappear."

Max opened his mouth but quickly covered it, pretending to stifle a yawn when Titus looked his way.

Mister Fowler expanded his throat and let out a long, loud, annoyed *croak*. He glowered and waited until he had the leaplings' undivided attention.

"Listen to me," he shouted. His already large eyes became even larger as he leaned over and pierced the leaplings with a sharp and desperate demand. The chatter stopped. "The Hoppernot has an evil weapon – a cold, ugly thing that makes a noise so loud you want to hibernate. A weapon so powerful it can—and has—dropped birds in flight."

"The Hoppernot is a sneaky creature. It disappears for long hours, but always returns – silent and unexpected. We, the Anura and all of the animals of Lake Fibian, dread those days the most. When the Hoppernot is here, it can be watched, but when it disappears—" Mister Fowler shuddered. "We never know when it will sneak up and snatch one of us away.

That is why we tell this Croaklore. That is why we must be careful. We do not know when the Hoppernot will return. If it will return. The Hoppernot is a master predator and one we do not understand."

Gripping the edge of the leaf, and with all the strength and persuasion he could muster, Mister Fowler impassioned, "A Hoppernot should never, ever, *ever* be approached or trusted." His large eyes blinked rapidly. "Our survival depends on it."

At the front of the crowd, a lone shaking hand rose up in the air. It was Benny, a leapling who recently lost his tail.

"Is it *really* that bad?" Benny asked. He glanced over to *The Three* hoping to catch their attention with his brave question, but they were whispering again.

Benny looked up at Mister Fowler and nearly swallowed his tongue when he saw the Elder frog's fierce frown. Benny lowered his eyes and glanced around, noticing the strange looks from the older frogs, especially the stern frown from his mother. He became even more uncomfortable when he saw the unsmiling faces of *The Three* who were staring at him now and clearly not impressed.

Benny hunched his body downward and wished he was a burrowing frog rather than a tree dweller.

Mister Fowler bit his tongue to prevent the angry retort he wanted to make. He understood the young frog was excited and eager to make a good impression with the other leaplings, but he needed to impress upon him, on all of them, the need for caution. With a single leap of his short legs, Mister Fowler landed on the ground.

He laid his hands on his wide hips and looked over at Titus with a quirked eye. He needed help and no one was better at it than Titus.

Titus' eyes swung left and right. He was scared, but he had to ensure the safety of his community instead of succumbing to his own fears.

"We must come together and protect Lake Fibian," Titus bellowed to the crowd. As Chief of Security, his word was law. The response to his announcement was quick and loud. *Claps*, *chirps,* and *croaks* sounded off all around the lake in agreement.

"Maybe they've left already," Mister Webster said. He was a peace-loving frog and hoped to calm some of the more excitable frogs.

"We can't take that chance," Mister Fowler replied, and then muttered, "As it is, they may have been here before today and we never knew. "

Some of the frogs closest to Mister Fowler heard the strange thought, but before the crowd could spread the words or ask more questions, Titus spoke.

"We must have lookouts in place to know when they return. Once we know why they are here, we can figure out how to get rid of them."

Max perked up and started to bounce in place. There was a twinkle in his eye. Spyder bit back a croak. He knew that look well and hoped Max wasn't getting any ideas that would get them into trouble.

"Critho . . ." Spyder was about to warn Cristobel, but one look at her and an unhappy croak escaped when he realized she too sniffed adventure in the air.

Cristobel stared straight ahead ignoring her friends and the crowd. Her white eyes widened as her horror and excitement grew.

Max bounced into Cristobel. He stepped on her toes and brought her attention back to her surroundings. She became aware of Max's excitement and the fact that Spyder tried to slip away. Cristobel grinned and listened carefully.

Mister Fowler raised his webbed hands to the crowd to stop the flood of questions.

"What about the Concord Pact? Should we sound the alarm?" Spyder asked, taking one step, then another away from the crowd.

"No, not yet. Most of the other animals have not returned from the Deep Sleep and we, the Anura Elders, do not want to cause unnecessary panic until we have all the facts."

Mister Fowler's eyes sought out as many of the Elders as he could see to ensure they all agreed. The last thing he wanted was wide spread panic. He didn't want to think of what could happen if the entire Anura panicked.

He scratched his throat. "I hope we have a day or two before we have to do anything as drastic as sound the alarm. By then, the Hoppernots will either be gone or the majority of our allies will have returned. Otherwise, I don't know what we will do."

"That's all we know right now," Titus spoke up. "The Elders need to gather and talk. When we come up with a plan we'll sound the Anura alarm and meet back here. Until then, be careful. Remember, we are family. We need to watch out for one another."

Mister Fowler and Titus stared at each other for a moment. They hopped away, speaking in low, worried voices. The rest of the Elders followed behind. The crowd around the lake fled to their homes.

All except for three small frogs.

three

Great Daring . . . or Simple Foolishness

"Worry Wart Wally is at it again," Max announced.

"What do you mean, Max?" Spyder asked.

"I doubt he saw anything at all," Max chirped.

Max hopped side to side. His eyes scanned the area. "How many times has he said he saw something no one else has seen? He's the nervous type and he's been hanging around Miss Milly lately; maybe she's rubbing off on him."

"I don't know about that Max," Cristobel responded. "He told the entire Anura. I think this is serious."

"Serious smerious. I don't believe it." Max sat back on his hind legs and crossed his arms. "Mister Fowler was the only to one to see them. Titus was with him and *he* didn't see the Hoppernots."

"I think—" Spyder began.

"Not only did Mister Fowler claim to see them," Max interrupted, "He said there were four of them. How come no one else saw the Hoppernots? Not a single frog sounded an alarm. If Hoppernots are here someone should have sounded an alarm."

"It's the beginning of spring so there are few animals around Sprocket Point House," Cristobel answered. "Mister Fowler has to inspect the house before everyone comes back from the Deep Sleep since he's the president of the Sprocket Point House committee."

She looked around, then focused her eyes upward and searched the shadows. "Hardly anyone hangs around there before the leaves bloom. Frogs were either here at the lake or on their way here for Luna Light Night, and most of the other animals haven't come back from their winter retreats yet."

"That's twue," Spyder nodded. "My mother likes to swim in the waters awound there and twies to get there early to avoid the cwowds."

Max and Cristobel stared blankly at Spyder. Neither of them understood what that had to do with anything.

"What about the birds or the squirrels? Why didn't they send out the alarm?" Max asked.

"Most of the birds haven't come back from their other homes and we all know how lazy squirrels are after winter," Cristobel replied.

Spyder nodded, "That's twue, too."

A sly look crossed Max's face. Spyder took a step back hoping to leap away in the opposite direction toward home before Max could make a suggestion he knew he wouldn't like. Max grabbed Spyder's arm before his back foot touched the ground.

"Why don't we go to Sprocket Point House tomorrow morning, early, and look around for ourselves? I bet we don't see any Hoppernots," Max suggested.

Spyder slumped. "I hate when you sniff out a new adventure."

Max stuck his tongue out at Spyder.

"Well," Spyder grudged, "Maybe not hate, but I don't want to go to Spwocket Point House. I don't want to see any Hoppewnots. My gwandmother told me they're big and scawy."

Max nudged Spyder with his elbow, then taunted, "Aw, come on scaredy. If it's true, which I doubt, but if it is, we can figure out what they're doing and tell the others. You heard what Titus said and you know how scared everyone is. No one will try to get close enough. They're too afraid of getting tadnapped and taken away."

Spyder scrunched his face and crossed his arms.

Seeing Spyder's uncertainty Max wheedled, "Aw, come on Spyder-man. I doubt we'll see anything at all."

Cristobel turned and put her hand on Spyder's shoulder. "We have to help, Spy," she said gently. "We have to. That's what Luna Light Night is all about. We take care of each other. We might be in danger, all of us."

"The Anuwa needs us." He sighed and rubbed the pads of his fingertips together. "Ohh, alwight. I'll go, but I weally don't want to."

"Come to my house in the morning," Max said. He bounced back and forth before he hopped toward his home, then stopped and called out to them.

"Don't let anyone know where we're going."

"Goodnight Spy," Cristobel said as she, too, hopped toward home.

Spyder stayed where he was, twisting his fingers together. "Why is it every time we do something that gets us into big twouble he always says those words?"

He stood on the lake's shore for a few seconds more. He looked up at the moon and closed his eyes against the bright light. Sighing deeply, he mumbled, "I hope we're not making a big mistake."

With another belly-deep sigh, he turned toward the moonlit path that would take him home, but he stopped in mid-hop. An uneasy twitchy feeling crept over his right leg. It felt as if he was being watched and his leg never lied. Looking around one last time, he hopped toward home.

four
Croak Blowing

Cristobel could not sleep. She was up long before her mother, who was an early riser and who was downstairs making a big hearty breakfast for her father and four sib-leaplings. Cristobel stayed in bed listening as she rustled around in the cookery.

Cristobel stared at the mellow yellow ceiling of her bedroom and tried to figure out how she was going to leave. She needed to leave fast, but not too fast, in case her mother became suspicious. She needed a plan that wouldn't result in her mother forbidding her from leaving.

When Cristobel stepped into the cookery she still didn't have a plan.

The cookery was a cozy room, covered with old red, yellow, and orange leaves and within the ridges of the oak tree they lived in acorns shells, which they used for preparing and serving her favorite meals, were tucked away.

"Hi Mama," Cristobel said with a bright smile.

"Good morning, Bel," Notty said, leaning over to kiss the top of her daughter's head. "You're up early. How did you sleep? No nightmares, I hope."

"Nightmares? Why would I have a nightmare?" Cristobel asked innocently. She grabbed an acorn with tiny fern leaves pressed on it and filled it with dunderberry waffles and mosquito dumplings.

As she squatted down to eat, Cristobel said, "Oh. You mean because of the Hoppernots."

Her mother looked sharply at her, but only said, "Yes, the Hoppernots."

"No, I didn't have a nightmare. I dreamt I was swimming with Max and Spyder and then we took a long nap by the bubbling pond."

"I want you to be careful, Cristobel," Notty warned.

Cristobel's mother rarely called her by her full name unless she was worried, or what she was saying was important.

Notty continued, "With the Hoppernot sighting—"

"Do you think it's true, Mama? Do you think the Hoppernot is back?"

"Mister Fowler and Titus would not have said so if it wasn't true."

"I don't know," she said, playing with her food.

"Mister Fowler is the Mayor. He would not have told the entire Anura if it weren't true. We need to be careful so until we know more, I want you to stay . . ."

Julius, Cristobel's father, walked in and stopped the flow of her mother's decree.

"What's for breakfast?" he asked.

Cristobel, seeing her chance for a quick escape, jumped up from the kitchen table, grabbed a sack, a napkin and her dunderberry waffles, kissed her father's check and said, "I'm-meeting-the-boys-at-Max's-house-we're-working-on-a-project-for-school-and-need-to-get-started." She took a deep breath as she rushed out the door, "I'll be very, very, very careful. Don't worry, Mama. Bye Papa."

"Cristo—" but the bark door shut before Cristobel could hear her mother call her back.

Lucky for Cristobel, she was a fast hopper.

By the time Cristobel met up with Max and Spyder, the early morning sky was changing from its pink and purple hues to a cloudless blue. They sat high up in a tree overlooking Sprocket Point House.

The morning was quiet. They were alone.

On the way to the lookout spot, they had to hide several times when a number of Elders hopped toward the lake, talking excitedly and plotting out the day's mission of finding out about the Hoppernot invasion.

Invasion.

They heard that word spoken by the passing Elders. That word, and the obvious fears of the Elders, caused the trio to move with more caution toward Sprocket Point House.

While they waited, Cristobel told them about the near miss with her mother, and then they sat in silence, watching the house and scanning the surrounding area.

"I heard the Hoppernot has legs as thick as trees and stomps-stomps-stomps around kicking fish and squashing moles," Max whispered to his friends, who muffled their giggles behind their colorful four-fingered hands.

"Well, I heard the Hoppernot has skin so thick and dry it flakes off in the breeze and suffocates ants when it falls to the ground," Cristobel added.

"I heard it talks funny," Spyder chirped up; his two friends laughed out loud.

"Shh," Cristobel said. She covered her mouth, trying to wipe away her smile. "We're being too loud. This is serious. We're supposed to be serious."

Max and Spyder looked at her, then at each other. They shifted their bodies, back to back and resumed looking around.

A few minutes later Spyder said, "I'm hungwy."

"You're always hungry," Max replied. His own stomach flipped with hunger as Spyder's belly protested its wait.

Cristobel gasped and jumped up. "I forgot. I have dunderberry waffles." She pulled them out of her four-leaf clover sack and shared her uneaten breakfast.

Spyder grinned. "I had the best flytwap stew last night." He smacked the rim of his mouth with his pinkish red tongue. "Miss Milly may be as nervous as a hummingbird, but she sure can cook."

"You're going to be as big as Kane the Toad if you don't stop eating so much," Cristobel said, sitting between the two. She stared at the house, looking around for movement.

"I love coming here," she whispered.

"Oh yeah, sthpeaking of coming here," Spyder said, "I think I was followed. My leg started twitching something fierce and . . . "

"Shhhh." Cristobel hushed her friends and turned toward Webb Road, the main pathway to Sprocket Point House. "Do you hear that?"

"Hear what?" Spyder asked as he squeezed his black eyes closed. He tried to listen, but all he could hear were the two leaves near him slapping together because he was shaking so hard.

"All I hear are birds," Max said, looking up at the four newly arrived blue jays chirping their morning wake up song on the branches high above.

Noticing his glare, the birds sang louder.

"No, that," she paused, straining to hear the sound again. "It sounds like something's growling. It's getting louder."

The blue jays, hearing the unnatural sounds, flew away.

Before they could suck in a breath, three strange and slow-moving creatures came into view, stopping in front of Sprocket Point House.

Red, white, and black eyes bulged wide at the sight of the beasts below.

"Oh my, oh my, oh my," Spyder cried.

"What are they?" Cristobel's voice squeaked.

"I . . . I don't know," Max said. He was as stunned as his friends. "I've never seen anything like them."

"Are those the Hoppewnots?" Spyder asked.

"I don't think so, but I don't know what they are," Max replied.

"They look scawy," Spyder said, his bottom lip quivered.

"Look, they're opening their ears," Cristobel croaked.

The sides of the creatures opened. The trio watched in silence as hard-shelled wings creaked open, revealing holes in the side of the creatures' body and six two-legged creatures emerged.

"Oh my, oh my, oh my," Spyder said, shrinking back. His dark blue fingers gripped the branch, turning them a lighter shade of blue.

"Wh-what are those things?" Cristobel asked, unable to tear her wide eyes away from the scene below.

"I don't know," cried Spyder.

"They're real," Max whispered, stunned at the truth before him.

"Are they what I think they are?" Cristobel asked.

Spyder tried to speak, but couldn't say a word.

"That's them all right. They look like my grandfather's description of the first Hoppernot. I always thought he made it up to scare me. I thought they were all making it up," Max said in awe, watching as the creatures moved around the house.

"Hoppernots?" Cristobel whispered, not wanting to believe what she saw before her.

"Hop . . . Hoppewnots?" Spyder chirped. He looked as if he were going to faint. For the first time in his life, he was not hungry.

"Listen," Max said. "They're making noises."

Below them, they watched the Hoppernots walk around the property inspecting the abandoned house and surveying the surrounding land. They watched as two of the Hoppernots tried to open the front door. It was stuck.

The Hoppernots pushed hard against the wooden door until it flew open. They ducked as disgruntled bleary-eyed birds flew at them from inside. The birds soared through the air toward the trees squawking their displeasure.

To the surprise and horror of the three in the tree, four new Hoppernots appeared from the rear of the house.

five
The Hoppernots

"The Hoppernots were two legged, two armed, wobble-headed creatures whose low, guttural sounds were indecipherable to the frogs hidden in the tree. Some of the Hoppernots had brown, black or yellow tufts of fur on top of their heads. Others had hard looking shells that looked to protect against things falling from the sky. There was one Hoppernot whose top looked like a smooth, shiny egg.

Their bodies were covered in weird, heavy looking material that either blew in the wind or stretched tight over their quick moving bodies, revealing the different shapes they came in. They ranged in colors from a pale cream to dark walnut. They were short and tall and plump and thin.

"Do you think the Hoppewnots come from different species like fwogs do?" Spyder whispered.

As the Hoppernots spoke, Cristobel hushed her friends and listened in fascinated horror as their voices rose and their guttural words began to make sense.

"Wow."

The first of the two-legged creatures spoke. The black tufts of fur on its head stood up like an irritated porcupine. "I thought the house looked bad last week, but it's worse than I thought. Well, Smith," the Hoppernot shook its head at another of its kind standing near it, "we have a lot of work to do."

The other Hoppernot was short, round and covered in a tan and green overall. It looked like a soft-shelled turtle. It paced back and forth and looked over the three-story house with a critical eye. When it spoke its voice was low and gravelly.

"The structure looks solid. These old homes were built to last, but the neglect may have caused some damage we can't see."

The house was a large tumbled-down monstrosity. Over a hundred and twenty years old and originally a stark shade of white, but the years and weather turned it into a sick looking grayish-greenish color with massive chips and cracked wood. The house was trimmed in blue, but the washed out color was barely visible through the errant vines clinging its way to the pitched roof.

The Hoppernots walked around the front of the house kicking at the porch steps and testing the strength of the railings.

"What are the plans for the house, Smith?" the porcupine-headed Hoppernot asked.

The turtle-shelled Hoppernot flipped over something light and fluttery like large white colored leaves. It bent its head and spoke.

"Says here they want to get rid of the asbestos shingles. There's wood siding underneath that should be in good condition. Once we get the shingles off and the wood passes inspection we're going to paint the outside yellow, white, and green to blend in with the surroundings. They don't want the house to look out of place."

"The house is already out of place. It's the only one around for miles." The porcupine-headed Hoppernot scratched its spikes and wrinkled its bare face. "Do we have to put those hot suits and the masks on?"

"Yup. If we don't want to get sick, we do," the turtle-shelled Hoppernot said. "The house is old. It's been abandoned a long time. I'm sure it's filled with the asbestos poison and if we're not careful it can spread to the land and harm the animals."

The porcupine-head puckered its mouth and let out a high-pitched piercing sound. "That's a whole lot of work to be done."

"Yup, and that's only the outside."

"The house will have to be gutted."

"You're right. The kitchen is a rotted, moldy mess. There are cracks in the windows and from the number of nests, webs, and acorn shells scattered around it looks like it's been the living quarters for a number of animals.

"The—"

CROAK.

The porcupine-head Hoppernot looked around and shuddered. "What kind of animals do you think are in there? Ugh, I hate rodents."

"We're in the woods, man," the turtle-shelled Hoppernot laughed. "Every animal you can think of is out there." It turned back to the house. "Anyway, I think the outside looks worse than it is, but it'll be a lot of work. We're lucky we've got a large crew this time. We should be able to finish this up in a few weeks if there's no slacking."

"I thought this was going to be a small cabin, not a three story mini-mansion." The porcupine-headed Hoppernot shook its head and with the sun glinting off the spikes, its faux quills looked wet and spiky. It groaned. "I don't even want to think about the inside of the house."

Two more Hoppernots came around from the back of the house.

"Why would anyone want to live out here, anyway?" A tall, bald Hoppernot with a barrel chest and long arms, asked. "There wasn't even a drivable road until we cleared out the bushes and made one. There's nothing out here but mosquitoes and silence."

"Well, Hank," said a Hoppernot wearing a soft blue helmet with what looked like a duckbill extending from its forehead, "some people don't like living in cities with fast foods and faster cars."

"Hunter's right," Chase, the porcupine-head said. "This place will be useful for the people moving here. They're scientists and study trees or frogs or something."

"Yeah, frogs," Hunter, the duckbill-headed Hoppernot said. "There's supposed to be something special about this place."

"I met the family who owns the house," the turtle-shelled Hoppernot said. "They told me the animals in this area are unusual. There's species living here that shouldn't be found in this part of the world. They don't know how most of them got here, but they plan to research it."

"Hey, there's a lake not too far from here," the duckbill-headed Hoppernot interrupted. "I'm sure the area is overrun with frogs and fish."

"I bet there's trout or bass in that lake. Maybe we'll have time for some fishing." Porcupine-head grew excited and raised his fist in the air.

"There's my slacker," the turtle-shelled Hoppernot said good-naturedly and ruffled the other Hoppernot's black spikes. Walking over to a large square shaped contraption, he pulled out a long, heavy looking limb with different shaped objects – some long, some short, some sharp and some blunt – that dangled all around it and shined in the sunlight. The Hoppernot wrapped it around its mid-section and locked it in place.

"I don't think we'll have time for anything other than work," the turtle-shelled Hoppernot said, his voice firm.

"You better forget about fishing." The bald one scratched his chin. "We haven't even looked inside yet. I bet it's a bigger mess than it is out here. Let's go look around the back and then head inside."

The Hoppernots walked away and was out of sight but their voices drifted up to the three in the tree.

"I wonder if these people will do experiments on the frogs," the porcupine-head said. "I remember I used to have to cut them up and look at their guts in science class. It was disgusting and pretty cool."

"I never liked dissecting frogs, but you know what I did like?" the duckbill-headed Hoppernot said.

"What?"

"Eating frog legs. They're delicious."

SIX
Ribbit What?

"They eat frog leg?" Cristobel cried. "They want to eat our legs? What kind of monsters are these?"

Max and Spyder exchanged shocked looks.

"And they think Sprocket Point House is a mess," Cristobel continued. "A mess. Sprocket Point House is the most beautiful place around the whole lake."

She rubbed her shaking hands together. "How could they say it's a mess *and* want to eat our legs?"

Cristobel missed her friends' reactions as she stared at Sprocket Point House.

Before them stood the same three story house, but where the Hoppernots saw an abandoned ruin, Cristobel saw a beautiful getaway where she and the other animals of Lake Fibian could relax and play together.

What appeared to be broken windows to the Hoppernots were doorways for animals to enter and exit onto different floors of the house. Spider webs were the artistic gifts of the different arachnid clusters. The holes in the roof let the sun shine through the house to warm the rooms or sometimes caught a breeze to sweetly lull the occupants to sleep. The birds and other climbing creatures who liked to leap down from the trees to enter Sprocket Point House used the holes as doorways. The mold and clinging vines were the earth's way of beautifying the house and embracing the non-nature made structure.

Cristobel let out a little chirp of appreciation.

"You . . . you understand them?" Max's voice filled with awe.

"Yes," Cristobel asked bewildered. "Didn't you?"

"No. Not a word." He turned to Spyder. "Did you understand what they said, Spy?"

"No, but I was too sca-wed to listen. I don't want to go missing like the fishies."

"The fish don't have anything to worry about. One of those *things*," she pointed to the retreating back of the Hoppernots below, "said they wouldn't have time to go to the lake."

Her eyes darted to the front door of the house.

"They'll be happy to hear that," Max said in relief and slumped against the base of the tree.

"Yeah, the fish will be happy, but it's the rest of us who have to worry," Cristobel replied.

"Wh. . . What do ya mean?" asked Spyder.

Cristobel said, "I think we're being invaded. One of the Hoppernots said there are something called Pee-ple moving into Sprocket Point House."

"What?" Spyder gripped the branch even tighter.

"What's a Pee-ple?" Max sat up straight.

"I don't know. They didn't say, but that's not the worst part," Cristobel said, her white eyes sad and scared.

"There's worse? What could be worse than Hoppernots and now Pee-ple?" Max asked.

"Not the bad part?" Spyder croaked at the same time.

"The one with the duckbill on its head – oh goodness, we're going to have to warn the mallard species too, you know how proud they are of their bills—well, it said the Hoppernots would be looking for us."

"For us? Why, what did we do?" Spyder asked, ready to spring off the tree or faint.

"What do you mean?" Max asked.

"The Anura are in danger. More Hoppernots are coming and they'll be looking for us and . . ." she gulped as huge tears appeared in her eyes. "We'll disappear like the fishies."

"And," Cristobel gasped causing her fleshy throat to wobble, "one of them likes eating frog legs."

"What?" Max exclaimed. His loud croak pierced the air.

"Why would they do that?" Spyder asked. "We hop with our legs."

"Shhh." Cristobel cautioned. "They might hear you."

"We have to go," Max rushed to say. "We have to warn the others. We need to sound the Anura alarm."

He started hopping up and down.

"Oh my, oh my, oh my," Spyder cried.

"Come on, let's go tell the others," Cristobel said and began hopping down the tree to the ground.

"Wait," yelled Spyder.

"What is it?" asked Max, eager to be on their way.

"We can't hop down there. We have to be caweful. We have to leap from twee to twee."

"Good thinking, Spy," Cristobel said.

Off they went, croaking the Anura's warning call as they bounced and leaped through the trees.

When the other frogs heard the croak blow, they too sounded the alarm until every frog was called and appeared at the far side of the lake, opposite of where they held the Luna Light Night festivities.

This side of the lake was denser with trees and vegetation. Plenty of places to hide or, if they were lucky enough to have the ability to change the color of their skin, camouflage themselves. From this direction, beyond Lake Fibian's perimeter, they would find other lakes and ponds if they needed to flee. It would be dangerous to do so, but a Hoppernot would be catching the bigger danger.

Frogs from every species and every lily pad or burrow surrounded the lake high and low. Even frogs under the water and the ones who usually stayed home until the evening showed up. The excitement around the lake grew. So did the fear. Sounding the Anura warning croak was serious.

"Who sounded the alarm?" cried Mister Fowler. He dashed about, hopping and leaping around, looking for the croak blower.

"Who sounded the alarm?" he asked again, when no one answered. "Who . . ."

"We did Worry War . . . uh, I mean Mister Fowler," Max yelled. He, Cristobel, and Spyder leaped to the ground.

"What's wrong?" Titus bellowed at them. His dark skin shimmered as water dropped off of him to the ground. Titus was responsible for sounding the underwater alarm.

"We came from Spwocket Point House," Spyder panted, trying to catch his breath. This time, for the first time ever, he was able to keep up with his friends.

The crowd gasped.

"What were you three doing there?" Titus demanded.

"We told everyone last night to stay away from there until we found out what was going on," Mister Fowler said sternly.

Mister Fowler always spoke sternly to Cristobel, Max, and Spyder. *The Three* had a bad habit of falling into situations that lead to trouble and he was the one who usually caught them.

"We know, but we thought we could help," said Max.

"It is too dangerous and you three are too young and reckless to be much help," Titus said, glaring down at them.

Indignant voices rose around the lake when the rest of the Anura found out the identity of the croak blowers.

"But we saw them," cried Spyder, hopping to the front of the group.

"You saw who?" asked Mister Fowler.

"The Hoppewnots," Spyder's twisted words whispered on the air, afraid to say the word out loud.

"What did you say?" Titus bellowed at him.

"Yeah, we can't hear you," cried a voice from the water.

"HOPPEWNOTS!" Spyder yelled toward the lake and fainted at Mister Fowler's and Titus' webbed feet.

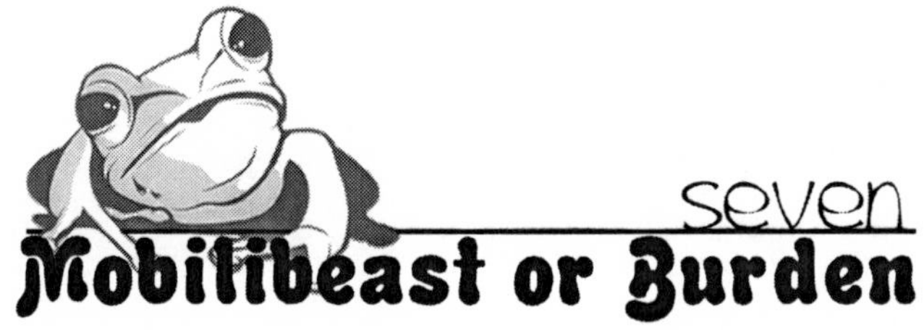

seven
Mobilibeast or Burden

Frightened gasps rippled around the lake when the crowd realized *The Three* had put themselves in danger. Two frogs standing close to the water's edge grabbed a few floating fern leaves and hopped over to Spyder. Laying the leaves down to form a soft bed, they picked Spyder up and laid him down.

"Out of the way, I say," a gruff voice demanded. Doctor Tom, a large, ruby red Tomato Frog, pushed through the crowd to reach Spyder. He threw his arms in the air to disperse the concerned frogs nearby and bellowed, "Let me tend to my patient, please."

Digging into his orange and purple bag, he pulled out a stalk of stinkweed and waved it under Spyder's nostrils. Spyder's eyes popped open and began to water from the pungent stinging scent.

Spyder moaned.

"What happened?" Spyder whispered, startled at the faces looming over him.

Doctor Tom did not hear his patient, and waved the stinkweed again, slapping it against Spyder's face, which caused him to squirm.

"I'm up, I'm up. No more of that awful stuff." He tried to get up from the leaves, but the doctor stopped him.

"Not so fast young man," ordered Doctor Tom. "You might be sick. You've been in contact with the Hoppernots. I need to check you before I let you go."

"I'm fine and we wewen't that close to them," Spyder replied quickly. He turned his body away from the stench of stinkweed and tried to stand up. "I'm sca-wed is all.

"I will be the judge of that." The doctor pushed his patient onto his back.

Restlessness rippled through the rest of the frogs who stood by waiting for details.

"Should we prepare to do battle?" a voice nearby asked.

Titus raised his hands, which trembled and said, "Let's not jump to conclusions, my friends. First, let us ask some questions."

"I wonder if the old Hoppernot who lived at Sprocket Point House was with them," Mister Fowler said. He turned back to Max and Cristobel.

"I don't think so, Mister Fowler," Max replied. "None of the Hoppernots had long white fur on their head or had skin with folds and cracks. They looked smooth like stones and there were at least ten of them."

"Ten Hoppernots, you say," Titus' booming voice rose to a louder pitch.

"Yes, ten of them," answered Cristobel, "and that's not all."

"What, leapling, what?" asked Miss Milly. She'd made her way to the front of the crowd and stood between Titus and Mister Fowler.

Spyder pushed Doctor Tom's hand away and said, "They didn't come alone. They came out of-of . . ."

Spyder looked over at Max and Cristobel for help, but they looked as bewildered as he was, so Spyder said the first thing that entered his mind.

"Mobilibeasts," Spyder whispered. "They moved in a way I've never seen before. Definitely beast-like.

Max and Cristobel bobbed their heads.

"I'm uncomfortable," Spyder complained. He tried to get up from his reclined position, but Doctor Tom, not so gently, pushed him back down.

"Mob…Mobilibeasts?" Miss Milly's voice squeaked.

"What is a Mobilibeast?" asked Mister Fowler, "And when and where did you see them?"

"We were in the tree in front of Sprocket Point House," Max began. "At first we heard a purring noise."

"Purring, did you say?" asked Doctor Tom. Doctor Tom looked down at Spyder and said, "That could have been my young patient's stomach."

Spyder rubbed his belly and scowled at Doctor Tom.

Max snickered then covered it with a cough.

"What did they look like and how many were there?" Titus asked.

"There were three Mobilibeasts—two big ones and a small one. Max rubbed his head. "They were blue, red and black. They had hard shells and they shined in the sun."

"They had the strangest feet I've ever seen," Cristobel added. "They were black with silver in the middle and they moved round and round instead of hopping, leaping, or picking their legs up."

"Even the Hoppewnots picked their legs up," Spyder added.

"Th-three," Titus sputtered. His throat clenched at the implications. "Hoppernots and Mobilibeasts."

"Okay, so there are three Hoppernots. Bad, but not too, too bad," Mister Webster said, his breath coming out in gulps. He was late joining the rest of the crowd and trying to catch up, but he confused the details.

"No," cried Spyder. "Not thwee Hoppewnots . . ."

"That's good." Miss Milly said and shook her green hopping shoot in the air. "We can run them off. They'll disappear like the other one did."

Miss Milly bobbed her head once as if that was indeed that and turned to go back home to prepare a snack, or most likely, take a nap.

A group of young frogs agreed with Miss Milly, forgetting the first Hoppernot had not been run off but chose to leave on its own.

"No, no, no. You don't understand," cried Cristobel. She hopped onto a rock, and then leapt to the lowest limb of the tallest tree she could find to get everyone's attention. When the frogs continued to talk amongst them, Max jumped up next to her, grabbed a hollow shoot and sent out a loud, piercing croak.

"Listen, all of you," he yelled into the weedhorn, which made his voice loud and easy to hear. "This is serious. There are ten Hoppernots and three Mobilibeasts."

As his words echoed throughout Lake Fabian, screams pierced the air. Nervous *croaks, squeaks, clacks,* and *clunks* sounded off from the farthest point of the lake.

"That's not the worst part," Max said, relieved to have everyone's attention.

"There can't be more." Mister Fowler wailed. "Please don't let there be more." The black spots on his dark green body grew as his breath quickened.

"There is." Max then remained quiet until he had the attention of every frog, tadpole, and toad. "The Hoppernots are coming after us."

"What do you mean?" asked Mister Fowler.

"How do you know?" Titus squawked. He rushed forward to stand underneath the tree limb. Titus looked more black than brown. Although he was large and one of the leading guards of the lake, everyone always knew when he was distressed. All black meant he was worried; all brown meant he was scared.

"Cristobel said so," Max replied.

A ripple of nerves tickled Cristobel's skin as every eye of every frog looked at her.

"Is this true Cristobel?" asked Mister Fowler.

"Yes, I heard them." She bobbed her head.

"What does that mean? Do you understand their language?" asked Seymour, a member of the Blue Poison-Darts. His bright blue and black speckled body swelled with suspicion.

"Y-yes. I understood them." She shrunk back and stood closer to Max. Although the frogs of Lake Fibian agreed to a truce, the Blue Poison-Darts were the one species everyone tried extra hard to keep the peace with. They were the least favored frog species and they knew it.

Cristobel bit her tongue, hesitant to continue. Max, sensing her distress, took her hand. He wanted to know why Cristobel could understand the Hoppernots, too, but he was willing to wait until they had less of an audience to ask her.

"Well? What did they say?" Sylvester, Seymour's brother, asked.

Cristobel grabbed the weedhorn and spoke, "The Hoppernots walked around Sprocket Point House. They said bad, horrible things about it and a few of them went inside."

"There goes our vacation spot," groused a Leaf Frog standing next to Miss Milly.

"And our homes, maybe even our lives," Miss Milly replied. The Leaf Frog's horned eyes snapped wide with horror. The thought of losing their vacation spot was maddening, but losing lives and homes was unthinkable.

"I don't know what they plan to do, but they said there would be more Hoppernots coming soon." Cristobel paused, her throat tight with tears. "They said something called Pee-ple are on their way too, but they didn't say what a Pee-ple was and. . ."

Cristobel couldn't speak another word.

"And? And?" asked Mister Webster, his voice rose. He stepped closer to Titus without realizing it.

"They're coming to the lake and they're gonna be looking for us," Spyder wailed. He fell back onto the leaves and passed out again.

This time when Doctor Tom waved the stalk of stinkweed under Spyder's nose, he didn't wake up quite so quickly. Doctor Tom, feeling curious and scared, laid a soggy Bluebell petal across Spyder's brow and stepped closer to the crowd.

"What are we going to do about this?" Seymour demanded.

"We don't know yet, we need to gather more information and we need to discuss it," Mister Fowler answered.

"Don't you Elders ever do anything more than talk?" Max groused. "We need to find out what the Hoppernots are doing at Sprocket Point House."

"The Hoppewnots are too big for us," Spyder said.

"That's why *we,"* he pointed to himself, Cristobel, and Spyder, "should be the ones to go back. We're stealthy. Titus can come with us."

Titus harrumphed, while Mister Fowler bristled at Max's impertinence.

"We can't do anything until we know what the Hoppernots are planning," Cristobel said.

"That means we have to go back," Max added with a big smile. Cristobel nudged him when the Elders glared at them. Max's smile disappeared.

Mister Fowler pushed off the ground with his long legs taking one large leap up to the limb Max and Cristobel stood on. He took the weedhorn from Max's hands and addressed the Anura.

"Ladies and gentlefrogs, I am afraid what we most feared has happened. Lake Fibian is being invaded and we need everyone's cooperation to, to . . ." he stumbled. His tongue became tied as worry and fright got the better of him.

"Make them go away," Max finished for him.

"Yes. Yes, we need to come up with a plan to make them go away. I will be forming a committee this evening, but right now we need volunteers to stand guard around Lake Fibian and croak blow if the Hoppernots appear."

Silence greeted his words. Even the grasshoppers, listening to the news, kept silent.

"If you don't volunteer," Titus' voice thundered, eyeing everyone within seeing distance, "I will pick you out whether you are willing or not."

Slowly, hands began rising into the air. Many of them trembled.

"That's more like it," Titus said and took a small dried out piece of bark with a soft black tip and a thin piece of white birch from his the pouch slung over his chest. He wrote down names and set up guard times.

"We'd like to help, too, Mister Fowler," Max piped in.

"I don't think so, son. Things could get dangerous," Mister Fowler said as he took a step to hop down to the ground.

"But we're the ones who alerted everyone to the danger. We sounded the alarm," Max cried.

"No, young man. It's too dangerous."

"We can do it, Mister Fowler," Max declared. "We're strong and fast. We may be able to out hop them."

"No." Mister Fowler started to move away.

"You may be bigger than we are, b-but you're old. You'll get caught. You can't move as fast as we can," Spyder piped in.

Eyes widened at the "old" reference and a few chuckles broke the ropes of panic paralyzing the crowd.

Mister Fowler grunted. He was about to say no again when Cristobel spoke up.

"So far I'm the only one who understands their language Mister Fowler," Cristobel said. "I have to go, but I want Max and Spyder to go with me."

"Where are your parents and grandparents?" Titus asked. "They need to be a part of this discussion."

"And maybe talk some sense into you," Mister Fowler added.

The trio watched as their family came forward and hotly argued against their involvement.

Spyder's family did not think he could move fast enough nor was he strong enough to fight against the Hoppernots.

Max's family argued he was only a leapling, barely older than a tadpole and he wasn't responsible enough to sense the danger.

Cristobel's father contended that since she was a girl leapling she could not be expected to sacrifice herself. Plus, she was the only daughter he had.

Notty, Cristobel's mother, stood silent. Her trembling fingers covered her mouth. She didn't know what to say, so she let the other families say all the things that would not come out of her mouth.

When the arguments stopped, the families of *The Three* looked around at all their scared family and friends and made the hardest decision of their lives. One by one, they bobbed their heads, blinking once, giving their permission.

"I have a question," Miss Milly said. "How do we know they're telling the truth? These three have been nothing but trouble since they lost their tails and now, just because they *say* Cristobel can understand the Hoppernots, we are going to believe them? What if they get hurt?"

"We have to take that chance," Titus said. "They know better than to tell fibs about Hoppernots. Isn't that right, leaplings? We are trusting you and putting our lives, all of our lives, in your hands. Do you understand the importance of our trust?"

"Yes, sir," each of the leaplings answered in turn.

Mister Fowler's sigh came from the deepest part of his stomach. His worried eyes drooped.

"They are much too young and too small to do much good, but," Titus huffed out a breath, "I think we need them. Cristobel may have what we need most, as well as the other two."

"What's that?" Miss Milly asked.

"The daring of youth," Mister Webster answered. He knew what he said was true because deep down inside he was a coward and secretly admired these young ones.

Miss Milly harrumphed and eyed *The Three* with weary misgivings.

"All right, but you three," Mister Fowler pointed at Cristobel and down to Spyder, then sent a warning glare at Max. "You have to do everything Mister Webster, Titus or I tell you to do. Do you agree?"

Max and Cristobel looked at each other. Max opened his mouth to speak, but another voice called out.

"We agwee," Spyder said. He was still reclining near Doctor Tom, but his color was normal and he looked like himself again.

"I don't think this is a good idea given your past troubles," Mister Fowler grumbled. He looked at the trio with a suspicious gaze, "But even I must admit we may need your help."

Mister Fowler leaped to the ground and hopped away. Mister Webster, Titus, and Miss Milly followed close behind.

Titus' voice drifted back to the leaplings. "Is it time to alert the Collaboration leaders?"

The response was lost in the wind.

Max and Cristobel joined Spyder at the edge of the water. For the first time in a long time, none of them had a word to say.

eight
Sprocket Destroyer

The next day Mister Fowler, Titus, and Mister Webster led the way to Sprocket Point House. The younger frogs followed behind, wide-eyed and twitchy. They stopped at a large rock before they approached Webb Road and the path that led to the front of Sprocket Point House.

The three Mobilibeasts stood quietly by the line of trees surrounding the house. They could hear the voices of the Hoppernots at the back of the house, floating down to them from open windows.

At the strange chatter Mister Webster jumped, bumping into a bewildered Mister Fowler.

"Is that them?" Mister Webster croaked. "Is that horrible sound them?"

Titus hopped around in a circle, making sure they were safe and alone.

"That's them," Spyder answered.

"Maybe we should leave?" Mister Fowler suggested.

"We can't leave," Max insisted. "Not yet."

"We should separate. It'll be easier to escape if we need to," Cristobel suggested.

"Good idea," Titus said, taking charge. "Mister Fowler, you and Spyder go to the back of the house. Mister Webster, you stay in front. Cristobel, you and I will go inside."

"What about me?" Max asked.

"Go up into the tree you were in before. You can be the lookout and warn us if you see any Hoppernots sneaking up on us."

"Okay," Spyder said. He hopped from one leg to the other. "Okay." He said it again, but firm this time. It wasn't okay, but it was all he could think to say.

"What signal should we use to warn if we're in trouble?" Max asked.

"How about *clunk-chirp-clunk-clunk-chirp-clack*?" Titus suggested.

"That works."

"We should look awound to see where the Hoppewnots are before we sthplit up," Spyder suggested.

"Good idea, Spyder," Titus approved. "Why don't you three hop up into the tree and we'll stay down here and look around."

Max, Spyder, and Cristobel climbed until they reached the same tree limb they sat on before. Cristobel, being the lightest, sat near the tip of the branch. Her eyes grew round and twitched at every sound.

"How long do you think we'll have to . . .?"

A loud bang from the second floor caught their attention.

The Hoppernot with the duckbill poked its head from a window on the second floor. A second Hoppernot, wearing bright red overalls and clunky black boots, opened the front door and stood under the window.

The duckbilled Hoppernot looked out the window again and began throwing things at the one on the ground.

The three in the tree gasped.

"What's it doing?" asked Max, amazed at the turn of events. "Do you think they're turning against each other?"

"I think it's angwy," Spyder said. He stopped speaking when the Hoppernot on the ground spoke.

"He's not mad," Cristobel said. Her eyes widened as she listened. "He's telling him to throw more stuff at him."

"Maybe he's cwazy," Spyder suggested.

"Oh no," cried Cristobel.

"What is it, Crithobel?"

"Look at what he's throwing out."

"Are those the wooden squares with the flat flowers you can't touch or smell? The ones that hang on the wall in the hall?" Spyder asked.

"Look, that's the tall, curvy stick with the smooth hard top that used to light up like a lightning bug's butt," Max said. "It's from my favorite room with the old, dusty doohickeys with the hard covers on the outside and the soft moveable wings with black squiggly lines inside. They have such a nice smell, too."

"You mean the things silverfish like munching on?" Spyder asked, then sighed. "Silverfish have the nicest crunch."

"Not now, Spy," Cristobel said. "Your stomach will have to wait."

"Oh no, Miss Milly is going to be vewy upset," Spyder said. He pointed at the round, rough ball that felt like it was stuffed with moss and covered in a strange blue, white and yellow skin and was now flying through the air towards the ground.

"She finally made her sweet spot in the center of it and now that Hoppernot is destroying it," Cristobel mourned.

"Why are they doing this?" Max wondered. He rubbed his damp hands against his cheeks.

"Shhhhh. They're speaking," Cristobel said. She edged closer to the tip of the limb to listen closer.

"Be caweful, Crithobel," Spyder cautioned.

"What are they saying?" Max asked. Both Hoppernots grunted as they threw and picked up the furniture.

"I'm not sure. I don't understand. I think they're speaking another language," she replied.

"Wow, how many languages do they sthpeak?" Spyder asked quietly.

"I don't know, but I hope they switched back to the one I understand."

They heard a loud croak from the ground, startling them. Titus waved them down. Taking deep breaths, Cristobel and Spyder hopped down to join the Elders, leaving Max alone.

nine
Closer. . . Closer. . .

Cristobel and Titus snuck past the Hoppernots standing outside the house. Cristobel's terror at being spotted was replaced by her shock at the destruction. As they moved deeper into the house the Hoppernot Croaklore replayed in her mind. A burning pit formed in her belly.

Cristobel glanced over at Titus and saw that he was as stunned as she was.

"They're destroying everything," she whispered.

The room was almost empty, proving the Hoppernots had been around far longer than the

Anura knew. The last time she had been there, the room was stuffed with large mismatched items she'd been told the Hoppernot used to use to sit and lay things on. Once the Hoppernot was gone a number of summers, and the animals began to feel comfortable that it might not come back, they transformed the rooms of Sprocket Point House into hidey-holes and an in-door bedding place they used to lounge on during the hottest times of the day.

"Things are changing faster than I imagined," Titus said. "Look over there."

He pointed to the two cracked entrances the Cricket and Spider colonies used to enter and exit the house. They were gone, replaced by hard shiny see-though shields with four square sticks that made a strange design. The flourishing vines, favored by the Squirrel Tree Frogs, no longer covered the walls and ceiling. Even the little pond—a round, metal item the Hoppernot used to bang on and make strange noises by the lakeside, which filled with water every time it rained—was missing.

Cristobel and Titus heard noises in the next room and hopped toward the opening to peer inside. They spied two Hoppernots in the emptied room with their legs folded in an odd angle, pulling the floor apart. A growing pile of wood lay in one corner. The towering two-door box that was one of the coolest places for animals to take a nap in was missing as well as the smaller matching box with the strange moveable knobs and four spiral circles on top. Cristobel looked up, closer to the ceiling and saw that the long rows of smooth wood that had held a few breakable items were also gone.

Titus beckoned Cristobel to retreat. They backed away as quietly and unobtrusively as they could.

"One of us should go upstairs and look around," Cristobel suggested. Titus, still in shock, turned toward the stairs, but before he took a step or tell her no, Cristobel said, "I'll go."

She flipped around and hopped up the stairs two at a time to the second floor, where four rooms were located. When she reached the top step, she stopped to catch her breath, not daring to look back at Titus, who was loudly hyperventilating behind her.

Cristobel hopped down the hallway as fast as she could. Two rooms were empty, while the other two contained Hoppernots either standing close to the walls raising and lowering their arms and causing the walls to change color with each movement or kneeling on the floor pulling and tearing up the ground. They worked silently each of them focused on their destruction.

She was about to creep out of one of the rooms when a Hoppernot picked up a floppy piece of greenery that looked like grass but was tougher and rougher against the skin, and threw it toward her.

A loud croak sounded behind her, making her jump out of the way, just in time to avoid the blow. It took Cristobel two leaps to get away from the danger.

Out in the hallway, Cristobel turned to Titus. She blinked watery eyes at him. She squeezed his hand, but said nothing. There was nothing to say.

Outside, Spyder and Mister Webster hid behind a tree stump shaking like tadpoles. Old Glory, as the stump was affectionately named when it was a fully-grown tree, led to the entrance the Bird and Squirrel species used to enter the house.

"The last time I saw Old Glory, she was a tree not a stump," Mister Webster said.

Spyder croaked sadly. "They must have come during the Deep Sleep."

"I hope not, Spyder. Otherwise we are in bigger trouble than we thought."

Spyder shuddered and looked toward Mister Webster for comfort, but he didn't find any. The rings on Mister Webster's back glistened and his eyes darted around.

"We need to remember as many details as we can to report back to the others."

Spyder gasped, then covered his mouth. He mumbled something, but Mister Webster couldn't understand him behind his closed fingers.

"Four Hoppewnots. Over there." Spyder pointed a shaking finger toward the Hoppernots looking up into the trees. Two of them pointed up at a tree whose branches reached over the house.

The Hoppernots emitted weird, guttural sounds. Spyder realized it was the language Cristobel understood. He squinted his eyes and listened. He hoped he could understand them and learn something useful to take back to the Elders.

"Maybe we should have taken this tree down, too," the brown straw-headed Hoppernot suggested. It moved its hands in a sawing motion and pointed to the spot where Spyder and Mister Webster hid.

"Naah, I think we should keep the tree, but trim back the branches," said a bald one. It pointed to the low hanging branches brushing against the roof, then shaped its hands like a cover.

"The homeowners will get some natural light in the daytime if we trim back the branches. They'll still have shade outside," another Hoppernot added, holding its hands over its eyes.

"Good idea. I'll go get the ladder," the bald one replied. It walked toward the same stump Spyder and Mister Webster hid behind.

"I think we're in twouble, Mister Webster," Spyder said. "They're either going to cut us in half, cover us up or blind us."

Mister Webster turned around and leaped into the nearest bush, causing a small brown sleeping sparrow to take flight as the Hoppernot came near.

Startled, the Hoppernot stopped right in front of the bush. Spyder was nervous, but he needed to do something to get the Hoppernot away from them so he let out low, throaty *chirp-clunk-clunk-chirp* sounds. The Hoppernot stepped back and away from the bush, walking around it in a wide arch.

Spyder took a giant leap and landed next to Mister Webster. He covered Mister Webster's mouth as he was about to croak and they both took a few steps backward, hitting their rumps against a tree.

With eyes closed, Mister Webster began to mumble. "I'm at the lake. I'm bathing in the sun. I'm not in a dangerous place. I'm safe. Safe."

The Hoppernot continued walking around the house and out of sight, while the other three kept talking.

Spyder was afraid their luck was running out.

How long do we have to stay back here, he wondered.

Mister Fowler was living up to the Worry Wart Wally nickname *The Three* called him behind his back. He had stayed in front of the house and was so terrified of the two Hoppernots standing next to the Mobilibeasts twenty yards - or six huge leaps - away, all he could do was squat and stare.

Mister Fowler harbored a secret.

Before yesterday, he never believed in the Croaklore of the Hoppernot even though he was one of the resident Croaklore tellers. He knew that more than a few of the Croaklores were tall tales and, as the young frogs guessed, the Elders created a few to keep then in line.

To Mister Fowler, the Croaklores were entertaining stories with cautionary lessons for the youngest members of the Anura. He even made up his own 'lores to tell and enjoyed scaring the leaplings. He never imagined he would ever see a Hoppernot in his lifetime.

He'd hatched the summer after the original Hoppernot left and the first time he'd heard the story about the Hoppernot was when he was a tadpole. But as mayor of Lake Fibian, the leaplings did not need to know he had never seen a Hoppernot.

The rest of the Elders, at least the ones who remembered that terrifying time, knew the importance of the Croaklores and vowed to keep his secret.

The need to protect the inhabitants of Lake Fibian was more important than his fear, so he expanded his lungs and with a rush of breath, did what he came to Sprocket Point House to do.

Taking a few steps away from his safe place, he looked around. He noticed that the largest Mobilibeasts were the same species but different colors: one was bright red and the other blue like the sky. The scariest of the Mobilibeasts was black with large white eyes trimmed with yellow. It was hard and shiny and, because Mister Fowler stood close to it, he could see and feel a fierce heat waving from its shell as if it boiled in angry displeasure from within.

The Mobilibeasts were quiet. Mister Fowler thought they were napping with their eyes open but he was afraid to get closer in case they woke up.

Two Hoppernots talked. One Hoppernot took strange things out of the ears of the red Mobilibeast.

The other Hoppernot pulled long pieces of wood out of the rear end of the blue one.

Swallowing his fear, Mister Fowler knew he needed to get closer. He wanted to discover if he understood the Hoppernot language. He was looking for a place where he could see, hear and hide, when he realized the Hoppernots had disappeared.

Spinning around in a circle he looked for them then crouched down low; his belly touched the ground. He crawled toward the high grass edging the woods, hoping the Mobilibeasts did not notice him.

High above in the tree Max watched horrified at how close Mister Fowler was to the strange creatures. Max twisted his hands together when the two Hoppernots reappeared and jumped into the black Mobilibeast's ears. A third Hoppernot, the one who'd caught the flying things tossed from the second floor, walked into the house.

Titus and Cristobel hadn't come out yet and Max was afraid they would be trapped inside.

"I have a bad feeling," he said, edging closer to the tip of the branch for a better look.

"Mister Fowler," Max called out. "I'm going up to see if I can find the others." Max looked at the branches above their heads.

"Be careful, Max," Mister Fowler called back.

Max flipped around and leaped on the trunk of the tree, making his way up. He looked through the tree limbs and out over the roof of the porch. On the opposite side of the house, tucked away under the shade of the trees, was an object shaped like a large, unnatural box.

"I wonder what that is," he mused, but before he could climb higher to get a better view, he heard a click and then a loud roar.

The black Mobilibeast was awake and it did not sound happy about it.

"Oh no," Max cried. He began hopping down the tree. "Mister Fowler," he cried. "Watch out."

But Mister Fowler could not hear him, the roar from the awakened Mobilibeast drowned out his voice.

The Mobilibeast's eyes flashed a bright light at Mister Fowler, targeting and mesmerizing him. As Max got closer, he knew Mister Webster was being hypnotized.

"Help," Mister Fowler cried.

Max saw Mister Fowler turn towards the woods and started hopping fast.

The Mobilibeast began to move. It picked up speed and raced towards Mister Fowler.

Mister Fowler was almost out of harm's way when the Mobilibeast let out three loud earsplitting bleeps. It was a sound unlike any either frog had ever heard.

The Mobilibeast stopped moving, but continued to purr, growling as if in anger at being awakened and impatient to be on the move.

Max let out his held breath.

The Hoppernot who entered on the left side of the Mobilibeast's body stuck its head out of the ear and called out. "We'll be right back. We're going to pick up some supplies and get something to eat. We'll be back in a few of hours."

"Okay, I'll tell the other guys. See you later," called down a Hoppernot who stuck its head out the front door.

The Mobilibeast roared again and shot forward.

Right over Mister Fowler.

ten
The Attack

Max watched the Mobilibeast drive away, leaving Mister Fowler lying stretched out on the ground. He lay unmoving, his pudgy body broken and still. Max forgot all about the agreed upon warning call and began sounding Code Hoppernot, the highest level of the Concord Pact alarm. He began alerting ever animal around Lake Fibian to the danger.

The power of his voice and the fear vibrating in his expanded throat carried the sequence of sounds making up Code Hoppernot—three sharp high whistles, two deep warbles, one long screech—

throughout Lake Fibian. Soon, he heard the echoes of sound being picked up and passed on, animal to animal around the perimeter of the lake.

Max waited until the Mobilibeast was way down the newly cleared road before he hopped to the bottom of the tree. He halted before jumping to the ground, not wanting to get too close.

For the first time in his life he was terrified all the way down to his webbed toes.

Max crept closer to Mister Fowler, then stopped to look around making sure the other Mobilibeasts stayed put. The last thing he needed was another unprovoked attack.

Mister Fowler lay on his back. His entire body began to shake. His chest heaved with deep, quick breaths and his eyes were closed tight. His left arm lay in an unnatural angle, his right leg unmoving and flattened. He moaned low in his throat.

Max sighed with relief. Mister Fowler was still alive.

"Mister Fowler, are you all right?" Max asked.

Mister Fowler didn't answer, but his low moan turned into a loud groan.

Max heard loud crashing noises in the tall grass behind him. Fearfully, he turned expecting to see a Hoppernot or another Mobilibeast charging at them. With relief, he saw it was only Spyder and Mister

Webster, and not far behind, Cristobel and Titus hopping toward him. They were all out of breath and looked frantic.

"What happened?" asked Titus.

"Why did you sound Code Hoppernot?" Mister Webster demanded.

"Was he attacked?" cried Spyder, who slumped against a tree, trying not to faint. He wasn't a fainter, but the arrival of the Hoppernots triggered something inside him and he could not help himself.

"Yes, the black Mobilibeast charged at him for no reason. No reason at all," Max said.

"Attacked? What are we to do?" Mister Webster asked.

"Is he . . ." Titus began, pointing at Mister Fowler.

"He's alive, but I don't know how badly he's injured," Max answered, "I just hopped down here, but I thought he was dead for sure."

"Maybe the Mobilibeast was warning him," Titus said.

Cristobel moved closer to investigate. Mister Fowler laid still and quiet. He had even stopped moaning. She feared the worst. She reached out her hand and was about to touch him, when he screamed, "HOPPERNOTS!"

Cristobel, Spyder, and Max jumped straight up into the air, each landing on a tree limb, shaken, but safely hidden.

Titus jumped into a nearby bush. He bumped his head against a rock, but he was too scared to notice the quick swelling and sharp pain.

Mister Webster laid flat on his belly. His wide webbed fingers covered his eyes. He removed his fingers, one at a time and scanned his eyes back and forth looking for Hoppernots. They were alone.

Mister Fowler tried to push himself up with his uninjured arm, but slumped back onto the ground and howled, rambling indecipherable words. He cracked open his eyes and lay with a confused look on his face, then focused on the swaying leaves above. He stopped moving. His chest rose and fell with quick shallow breaths. His dark green face grew pale and damp, while pain radiated from every part of his body.

"Mister Fowler, I say dear man, are you all right?" Mister Webster asked, his large eyes flitting around, making sure they were indeed alone.

"What? Who's there?" His voice was weak and pain-filled.

"We're up here," cried Max, waving his trembling hands. "Up here."

Looking up, Mister Fowler stared at each of them as if their brains had been shaken. "What, may I ask, are you all doing up there? We're supposed to spy on the Hoppernots. We need to separate; it will be easier to escape."

With cautious steps, Max, Spyder, and Cristobel walked, and then hopped, down the rough bark of the tree. Their eyes darted around, then toward the house and through the trees as they moved closer.

"Don't you remember what happened?" Max asked.

"Of course I remember," Mister Fowler wheezed out. "We were discussing where we were going to hide to gather information on the Hoppernots."

Looking around he asked, "Why are you staring at me? We have important things to do. Let's get to it."

The five of them looked at each other, eyes wide. Mister Fowler's voice was weak, but he didn't seem to remember the last few terrifying moments.

"I think we should take him to see Doctor Tom," Spyder whispered.

"Speak up, leapling. You know it's not polite to whisper in the company of others," Mister Fowler said.

He tried to roll over.

"Owwww," Mister Fowler cried. He lifted his right arm to grab his right leg and was about to use his left arm for leverage, but fell back on the ground. "I have a pain in my leg and my head hurts."

"That's not all you have," Max muttered, and then yelped as both Cristobel and Mister Webster elbowed him in the side. Max thought they'd appreciate his little joke, but they didn't see anything funny about the situation.

"Be quiet," Mister Webster hissed. "He doesn't know how badly he's injured."

"Come on, Mister Fowler. I think we need to get you looked at. We can come back later and . . ."

"We may not have time," Mister Fowler interrupted Titus, "we need to gather information fast."

"Now, Mister Fowler, don't worry," Cristobel said.

"That's wight," Spyder added.

"We'll help you get back to Lake Fibian and find Doctor Tom," Max croaked.

"Then we'll come back and continue, that is, we'll spy on them. Don't you worry about a thing," Titus added.

"Ohhhh, all rrrright," Mister Fowler said. "I feel a bit offff and I could use a nappy."

They noticed a slight slurring in his speech. Quickly, his eyes drifted shut.

Max and Spyder gently grabbed Mister Fowler and heaved him onto the backs of Mister Webster and Titus. It was obvious Mister Fowler's arm was broken by its unnatural angle, but a flattened leg was something none of them had ever seen before. They were afraid to jostle him and make his injury worse.

"His leg is as flat as a leaf pancake," Spyder whispered.

At Spyder's mention of food, Cristobel asked appalled. "Are you hungry even now?"

Spyder considered her question. "I'm not hungwy at all."

"That's almost as scary as the Hoppernots," Cristobel replied.

Slowly, they made their way to Lake Fibian. The younger frogs acted as guards in case of another attack.

It took three times as long for them to return to the lake. Mister Fowler was a bit on the plump side and Titus and Mister Webster were different sizes, which made it difficult to carry him and hop fast.

Leaping toward the lake would have been faster, but Mister Fowler yelped the first time they leapt, and so they realized it was a bad idea. It did not help that he passed out during the trip through the woods. The dead weight of his bulky body slowed their progress down even more.

Max and Spyder tried to help, but their smaller bodies couldn't lift Mister Fowler's bulk. They were all tired, out of breath and glistening when they arrived at the lake.

Finally, exhausted and happy to arrive safe, they laid Mister Fowler on a soft bed of moss, but before they could slump into exhaustion, they realized they were the last to arrive.

As they became aware of the crowds their tiredness fled. They stood in awe at the number of wide, wild eyes staring at them.

Noticing Mister Fowler's unconscious state, two Runner frogs of the Golden Mantellas, the bright orange colored species, went in search of Doctor Tom.

The end of the Deep Sleep was near. The animals who had come back to Lake Fibian from their yearly migration, awakened from hibernation or deep-sluggish nap-ins —the flocks of birds, warrens of rabbits, drays of squirrels, braces of ducks, bales of turtles, nests of snakes, parliaments of owls—and the other animals who inhabited Lake Fibian and had returned to the lake region during the night and early in the morning, were in attendance.

As they waited, the species present talked amongst their members. The murmured voices blended and increased everyone's fear. Those recently returned to Lake Fibian were curious and growing impatient as their questions remained unanswered.

The frogs who knew what triggered the panic, but not how or why, remained silent.

Nervous *squawks, squeaks, chirps, groans, growls* and *harrumphs* exploded throughout the gathering when the animals noticed the new arrivals. Everyone was afraid to stay in one place too long in case an attack was imminent, but they were more afraid to leave without finding out what triggered the use of Code Hoppernot.

"What's happened?" Miss Milly asked.

She pushed her way through the crowds. Her eyes widened at the number of Lake Fibian Collaboration leaders and the larger number of species present and in close proximity. She shrank down closer to the ground as she eyed the large winged and furry creatures standing nearby. Her vision blurred, so she fluttered her eyes rapidly and took a deep breath, filling her cheeks and lungs with much needed oxygen.

Spyder hopped next to her and grabbed her hand. He knew being so near the other, larger animals unnerved her and was sure the other frogs felt the same way, but Spyder knew Miss Milly didn't want to miss a single word and would save her fainting spell for a more convenient time. "I forgot today was when the Collaboration leaders returned," Miss Milly whispered to her nephew. She gripped Spyder's hand so hard his eyes watered.

Foster, a Bald Eagle and the leader of the eagle convocation drawled, "Did one of you sound the Code Hoppernot alarm?"

"If my hearing is correct, and it always is, why?" He asked in a deep, raspy voice.

Max, who was standing closest to the eagle, nearly groaned, but caught himself when Cristobel bobbed her head and blinked rapidly at him.

He sighed. It wasn't easy keeping his thoughts to himself, but luckily, Cristobel knew him well enough to prevent him from saying something he shouldn't.

"Where is my patient?" Doctor Tom bellowed, rushing through the crowd.

Three of his senior students followed. They were less careful in their rush and enthusiasm, which caused angry outbursts from the mixed crowd when they were pushed to the side or knocked down.

Foster turned a gimlet eye on them; however, being young, spirited and on their first official medical case, they ignored the big bird and continued to rush forward.

"Mister Fowler is over here, Doctor Tom," Titus answered. "He's lying down. He's hurt his leg."

"He got the bat-sense knocked out of him," Mister Webster whispered. He tried not to alarm Mister Fowler who seemed, while awake, unaware he'd been involved in a frightening altercation with a Mobilibeast.

"He doesn't remember the last few hours we spent at Sprocket Point House," Cristobel said.

Doctor Tom looked over at the unconscious Mayor. He swiftly noted the strange angle of his arm and badly injured leg.

Mister Fowler was so still Doctor Tom became alarmed. He jumped to his side and sucked in a breath when he noticed first a large, bloody lump on the side of Mister Fowler's head and then his flattened leg.

"I think we should move him to the Burrow. I can take better care of him there," Doctor Tom replied, hopping up and down.

"While I am always ready to heal a new patient," Doctor Tom said, turning to Titus, "there is a small, but selfish part of me that wants to stay and hear what's been happening. Alas, I have a duty to uphold the Hoppercratic oath. My patients come first. I guess I'll have to wait and learn what's going on around here."

"Don't worry, Doctor Tom," Titus said. "One of the Elders will come to the clinic later and fill you in on what is happening. We need to keep you informed."

"Thank you, Titus," Doctor Tom replied. "I seem to be getting busier now that the Hoppernots have arrived. I hope this doesn't continue." He turned and watched his students gently hoist their newest patient onto a twig and twine gurney and carry him away. The Golden Mantellas frogs followed closely to guard them against any more attacks.

"I'll have to recruit more of my students to help if this keeps up. I don't think they're ready to doctor so many frogs," Doctor Tom mused.

"Let's hope it doesn't come to that, Doctor Tom," Miss Milly replied, anxiously waiting for him and his patient to leave so they could learn what happened at Sprocket Point House.

eleven

The Concord Pact or What Do You Do When Your Elders Can't Get Along?

Once Doctor Tom and his patient were out of sight, Mister Webster called for order. He was the Deputy Mayor and second-in-command after Mister Fowler.

"Ladies and gentlefrogs of Lake Fibian, I have distressing news. As some of you are aware, we have been invaded." He paused and looked around to make sure he had everyone's attention.

"What do you mean invaded?" Foster demanded. "What in the name of lightning has been going on around here? I flew in less than half sunrise ago and I come back to chaos."

"I'm getting to it," Mister Webster snapped. Foster, the bald eagle was a bit of a bully. Mister Webster refused to let Foster rattle him.

"Some of you may recall the Hoppernot who lived up the hill at Sprocket Point House." His eyes scanned the crowd, connecting with the animals who had been alive during that dark time. "We were fortunate there was only one Hoppernot, and while it caused us many sleepless nights, it left many of the lake's inhabitants alone."

"Why is Mister Webster wambling?" Spyder whispered.

"Beats me," Max answered. "I wish he'd get to the point already."

"Shh, listen," Cristobel said. "There's noise coming from the water."

The sound of popping water bubbles surged from the lake. The wriggling of hundreds of fish bobbing up and down disturbed the normal placidness of the lake. There was one fish, leaping over and through the throngs. She stopped when she came to the lowest tide of the water and gasped, her sides heaved as she caught her breath from her hurried pace to reach the lakeside and find out if the rumors were true.

Mona.

Mona was a striking silvery Rainbow Trout who still mourned her brother who was taken away by the first Hoppernot. She had been swimming upstream with her brother Darius that long ago day when the unthinkable happened.

Everyone knew the story.

The Hoppernot entered the water holding a long handle contraption with a large netted sack on the end that looked like tightly spun spider webs. The Hoppernot stuck it in the water. Mona was its intended target, but her brother jumped into the net and pushed her out before it was pulled out of the water.

It was the last time Darius was seen alive and everyone understood that the strange burning smells coming from Sprocket Point House had something to do with his disappearance.

Mister Webster's throat inflated. "It is confirmed."

"What is confirmed?" Foster snapped. He ruffled his blackish-brown feathers and arched his brow. His piercing yellow eyes glared. "I think you forget most of us have just arrived. We don't know what's been going on to cause the use of Code Hoppernot—"

"Is it true?" Mona interrupted. "Has the Hoppernot returned?"

Mister Webster swallowed several times before he answered. The flesh under his chin sucked in tight and trembled, then expanded with a quick quiver.

"No, Mona. The Hoppernot we knew has not returned."

Mona slowly sank beneath the water, then resurfaced and let out a relieved bubble of air from her thin lips. Mister Webster's heart sank to his webbed toes. He wished he did not have to kill her sense of security.

"Get on with it, Mister Webster," Foster groused.

Speaking in a stronger voice, Mister Webster said, "It is not the same Hoppernot who terrorized us in the past. We are now being invaded by ten Hoppernots and things are far more serious."

Max stamped his foot. He was irritated at the hemming and hawing.

"That's not all. The Hoppernots brought along monsters," Max said. "Three Mobilibeasts who will attack for no reason."

Mister Webster heard Foster's beak click close.

"That shut the old, unbearable coot up," Mister Webster mumbled.

"What are Mobilibeastssss?" asked Alina, a large green and yellow Emerald Tree Boa snake. She hung down from a tall oak tree overlooking the crowd.

"Perhapssss my nessstssss of ssssnakesss can ssssqueeze them out of here?"

Hisses of agreement spread throughout the snake nests. A few forked tongues quivered a little too close to a family of field mice causing them to scurry away.

"What do you mean attack?" asked Tobias, a multicolored Painted Wood Turtle. Every turtle on land and in the water stuck out their heads, bobbing up and down.

"What are we to do?" asked Laramy. He was the leader of the Heron siege. Herons all around the lake shook their feathers indicating their readiness to fight.

"Did you see the Hoppernots?" Foster interrupted. "Where were they and when did they arrive?" As a bird of prey, he knew that having all the facts first was important to coming up with the perfect strategy.

"Yessssss, where are they now and how do you know how many there are?" Alina added.

Titus looked over at Mister Webster and noticed his fingers nervously digging into the earth. Titus knew the situation was too big a job for the frogs to handle alone, but this would be the first time all the animals of the lake would work together. They would have to rely on each other. Titus feared they would fail this first test; failure could result in someone's death. As one of the Anura leaders, it was not easy for him to admit his fears and reservations to this crowd.

Titus began by telling the animals the happenings over the last few days. He paused in the middle of his recital, hesitant to mention the involvement of Cristobel, Max, and Spyder given their reputations. Titus knew he had to reveal their part in discovering the Hoppernots, the new threat they brought with them and the surprising fact that Cristobel understood the Hoppernot language.

"How do we know thosssse three haven't been up to their usssual missssschief?" Alina asked. She slithered in close to Max and stared into his eyes, mesmerizing him with their dark intensity."Is thissss another one of your jokesssss?"

Max squirmed and heard Spyder mumble, "Why would we joke about Hoppewnots? We're not *that* bad."

Alina let out a long hiss. Her tongue flicked out and her knowing black eyes stared at Max. Although snakes were often loners, the nests kept each other well-informed on what was happening around the lake. Max had a feeling Alina already knew about the Limmon pit incident. He hoped this wasn't the moment that misadventure was revealed. They were in enough trouble.

"It better not be," Laramy said. He stomped his foot, shaking a few feathers off his long body. "I haven't been home yet. I would not appreciate one of their tricks and neither will the rest of the flocks when then hear about this."

To the discomfort of Cristobel, Max, and Spyder, heads turned, bodies rolled, flipped and contorted to look at them. They tried hard not to squirm under the hard-eyed stares, but it was difficult.

Spyder yelped and jumped forward as a sharp nip bit into his rear. A young snapping turtle, barely out of the water, looked around as if looking for the nip-snapper.

Mister Webster nudged Titus, prompting him to speak. Titus' voice was loud enough to be heard and strong enough to be believed. He opened his mouth to speak, but another voice, raised high in panic, yelled out.

"Benny? Benny, where are you?" A small brown Spring Peeper frog leaped through the crowd, stepping on toes and pushing frogs and leaplings over in her hurry. "Where are you?"

"What's going on, Ina?" Titus asked.

"Benny. He's been missing since early this morning. He snuck out of the house and I haven't seen him since." Ina stepped from foot to foot, eyes darting around trying to look through the crowd.

"Has anyone seen Benny?" Titus asked the crowd.

"No's and 'not since Luna Light Night' echoed back to them. Ina began to weep.

"What could have happened to him?" she wailed. "He's just a little leapling?"

In a slow, steady circle Mister Webster turned at looked at Cristobel, Max, and Spyder.

"What do you three know about this?" he asked.

"Nothing," Max said quickly.

"Nothing at all," Spyder added. "We didn't even see him at Luna Light Night."

Titus let out a loud tired breath. "We'll need to send out a search party. Don't worry, Ina. We'll find him."

"What if the Hoppernots got him?" she wailed.

He didn't know how to respond. Saying nothing to Ina, Titus closed his eyes tightly as she cried and other frogs closed in and tried to comfort her, while watching for strange movements in the distance. The other species stood by looking at one another not knowing what to think.

When Titus opened his eyes a few moments later he saw a few of the Golden Mantellas, Green Tree and Leopard Frogs standing clustered together. "I want you to look around the lake and up in the trees, and don't forget to talk to the fish. Maybe he decided to take a dip and forgot the time. You know how leaplings get sometimes."

"I'll send a few of the eagles with them," Foster offered.

A few of the other species offered to help and just as the search party was about to depart a squeaky voiced piped up.

"I'm…I'm here Mama." Benny hopped tiredly into the clearing. His eyes drooped with fatigue and fear.

Sighs of relief exploded in the air, until Ina screeched, "Where have you been?"

"I, uhh, I tried to followed Max, Spyder, and Cristobel to Sprocket Point House." He flinched at his mother's accusing gasp and glare.

"And the Elders. I was following the Elders too," Benny added, knowing everyone would blame *The Three* for being bad influences.

Angry eyes turned toward the silent trio, who glared back indignantly.

"They didn't know I was following them. I hid in another tree so they wouldn't see me. I wanted to watch the Hoppernots too, but then they," he pointed to Cristobel, Spyder, and Max, "sounded the Code Hoppernot. That's when I saw one of the Hoppernots near a tree. I wanted to see what it looked like and hopped closer. It…it tried to grab me, but I got away.

I was so scared I just started hopping and didn't pay attention to where I was going. I didn't stop hopping until I was deep in the woods. I think I was half way to the Basin of Taynt, and then I remembered that Croaklore about it and so I stopped. I stayed there in case the Hoppernot followed me but it didn't and then I fell asleep after that and…I just got back."

With a powerful leap, Ina landed in front of him. Gently she placed her hands on his arms and kissed the top of his head.

Then, taking a quick step back she yelled, "The Basin of . . . oh my, don't you ever do something like that again. I told you to stay away from *The Three*. They are nothing but trouble and what did you find but your own self in trouble. Just you wait until we get home. You won't see the sky until after the next Deep Sleep."

Grabbing Benny's hand, Ina dragged him away from the crowd and headed toward the safety of their home.

Benny's voice drifted back, "But they didn't have anything to do with me following them. I just wanted to see what a Hoppernot looked like."

Once they left, Titus and Mister Webster stepped closer. Titus gazed around. Most of the other animals had been quiet the entire time Ina announced Benny's disappearance. He hoped, if nothing else that would make them understand the dire situation they were all in.

"As you can see this is not a trick. Do you think we would have sounded the highest alarm of the Concord Pact if we were not sure?"

Titus took a deep, cleansing breath to calm his racing heart.

"I, as well as Mister Webster—both of us leaders of the Anura and members of the Collaboration—have seen the Hoppernots and the Mobilibeast monsters they've brought with our own eyes and the attack on Mister Fowler was real. All of us are in danger."

Titus heard Foster grumble beneath his breath, but now was not the time to quibble. They were facing their biggest threat and needed to keep their wits up and their fears under wraps.

A single Hoppernot was bad, but ten Hoppernots were unimaginable. Figuring out a way to protect themselves would take strength and focus. Fear and resentment had no place in planning out a battle.

"So," Foster began, "where do we go from here?" He was ready to sink his claws into action.

"Maybe we should leave? We can go back to our other homes," called down one of the hawks.

"We can go underground," said a small brown, blindish mole. "We can stay down there as long as it takes." The other moles nodded eagerly. Moles preferred to avoid conflict whenever possible.

"That's fine for you," exclaimed a protesting squirrel, her bushy tail twitched back and forth. "What about those of us who don't have second homes to go to?"

"Or who can't burrow underground or fly away," Thad, a cottontail rabbit added.

"You can't burrow, you twit," snapped Foster.

"I know I can't. We rabbits build them, we don't dig for them, but I was thinking of others. Unlike you." Thad's nose twitched as he sneered at the eagle. Thad scuttled around, putting his back to the big bird.

Angry outbursts and disgruntled grumbles spread through the crowd. The first coming together of the Lake Fibian Collaboration was turning into a disaster.

Cristobel, Max, and Spyder began flapping their arms and hopping up and down, going higher and higher into the air. The crowd watched their agitated movements in fascination. With a last hop they landed on a large craggy rock.

"Enough," Cristobel cried.

Max spoke up. "Why are you arguing instead of trying to come up with a way to save our lives? Stop fighting and start planning."

"We can't abandon our homes," cried Cristobel. "So calm down and talk to each other. We're dealing with Hoppernots. Now's not the time to bury our heads in the dirt. We can't pretend our problems away."

"Or argue about stupid stuff," Spyder chimed in.

"Why should we listen to you three? You're not members of the Collaboration," Seymour jeered.

"That's right. You should let the leaders do the leading," Sylvester, Seymour's twin agreed.

Other voices joined in the debate.

"This is turning into a debacle," Max groused.

"Be qwiet!" Spyder leapt into the air and bleated out the command. His unexpected outburst caused angry eyes to turn toward him, stunning the animals into silence; for once in his life, Spyder didn't allow disapproving stares to prevent him for giving his opinion.

Something else did.

For a brief moment, clouds dimmed the sunlight, and an eerie shudder rippled through the throng. In the uncomfortable silence Spyder heard the languid flapping of wings.

Twenty disreputable crows lowered themselves onto branches.

twelve
The Agreement

Mantu, the leader of the crows, had listened in silence and sent out a signal for his murder—the flock of crows he lived and traveled with—to join the rest of the Collaboration. His blue-black feathers glistened, looking wet, glossy and ruffled. His beady black eyes zoomed over the other crows as they cawed and screeched their findings.

The crows may have looked languid, slowly descending from their higher, hidden perches among the trees, but when Mantu noticed the ground disturbances upon their return to Lake Fibian, he grew suspicious that a predator was among the animals who had remained around the lake during the Deep Sleep.

Mantu's constant and intense vigilance was prized among the crows. The last thing he wanted was to walk into a trap, so hours ago, before he and his murder returned to their roosts, he sent out a command for the other crows to soar high above the trees and scout the surrounding area to find information and look for trouble while he quietly hovered close to the lake, keeping watch and listening to the arguing animals.

The crows had been at it for hours, circling the skies, hiding in trees, and gliding as close to the ground as they dared. They held back calling out to one another and met in small groups to pass on information to the rest of the murder.

When the crows settled on the swaying limbs of the trees surrounding him he sent out a single, silencing *caw* then focused his attention on the animals before him. He wasn't fond of the Collaboration. Most of the animals were predators and he didn't think it was natural to suppress one's basic instincts, but he was a smart crow who enjoyed living at this particular lake. The lake and the surrounding land, waterways and distant mountains were large enough so he and his flock did not have to leave and go to that scary place he had visited when he was young.

Swaying his head left and right, Mantu shook off thoughts of the other place, the place he chose to forget, where his vision had been obscured by fast moving unidentified objects that chased each other for no good reason. Flight paths were blocked by hard tall structures instead of trees. It was harder to find the foods he craved in that other place; for him making peace with the other animals at Lake Fibian was a small price to pay.

It was in that horribly cold, unwelcome place that he had first encountered the Hoppernots.

"It's Mantu," Cristobel whispered to Max, then reached over to squeeze Spyder's fingers, reminding him to breathe. Mantu was a legend, known as one of the fiercest warriors around Lake Fibian.

The Three watched in awe as Mantu settled his black talons on a low hanging branch and slowly perused the gathering. From their left they could hear the grumbling of some of the Collaboration members who looked scared at the arrival of the crow and hostile because Mantu's presence was able to do what no one else could.

He completely silenced the crowd.

"I hope he doesn't cause any twouble," Spyder whispered, or thought he whispered. The sharp-eyed crow turned his head and pinned Spyder with a baleful glare.

Max opened his mouth to say something, but was halted when Mantu lifted his right wing and said, "This explains the ground disturbances we've seen around Lake Fibian."

"What kind of disturbances?" Foster asked. He sniffed, he hadn't seen anything and he, of all the flying animals, would notice such a thing.

Mantu clicked his beak and stifled a grumble of laughter. It amused Mantu to tweak the eagle's confidence. Foster and his lot were an arrogant flock and Mantu liked nothing better than ruffling a few fine feathers.

"There are trees missing, rocks have been moved or realigned and there looks to be a new winding path leading to Sprocket Point House." Mantu looked Foster in the eyes with unblinking intensity. "I would call that a disturbance."

"Not possible," Foster harrumphed. "I would have noticed it."

"Only if your head weren't held so high with pride," Mantu replied silkily.

Foster opened his beak to respond, but Cristobel interrupted, "You two need to work together," she insisted. "Everyone knows you don't like each other, but can you put it away for awhile."

"Yeah, like right now would be nice," Max chimed in.

Both birds opened their beaks to respond, but Alina's voice cut them off before an argument began.

"Where did you ssssseeee thissss?"

"On the other side of Sprocket Point House, leading away from the lake," Mantu replied.

"Has anyone noticed anything strange going on over the last few Luna Light cycles?" Titus asked. "I know most of you go away for the cold season, but some of you who stay must have seen something? Heard something?"

Heads and eyes darted around.

A groundhog hidden behind a bush stepped out. "There were a few times I thought I heard a rumble and felt the earth move, but I thought it was the wind or maybe a fallen branch or two, so I went back to sleep."

"So did I," said a squirrel.

A few snakes hissed and other animals moved in ways that confirmed.

It hadn't dawned on any of them to leave the warmth and comfort of their homes during the cold, bitter months to check out a strange noise or quakes. In deepest slumber, anything not immediately threatening was ignored.

Titus hopped around in a small tight circle looking at the animals up in the trees, in the lake and those huddled on the ground. He was disgusted with the lot of them, but with himself the most. He, too, had heard and felt the odd activity going on and had kept right on sleeping. It was his job to ensure the safety of the Anura and he'd slacked off through it all.

"The Lake Fibian Collaboration was created for this reason," Titus reminded them. "I implore you all to listen to what we have to say. Someone has already been hurt."

A nervous grasshopper who could not stop his legs from rubbing together crossed them and held his feet to stop his worry song.

Cristobel, Max, and Spyder huddled together, silently listening to the Collaboration Leaders talk late into the night. Max wanted to chime into the conversation, but Spyder, in a hushed voice, suggested they let the older, wiser leaders do the talking.

Cristobel agreed. It was time for them to listen and not act on impulse.

Max agreed. For now. He knew if they drew attention to themselves, the Elders would send them home to their beds.

The animals continued the debates, arguments and pleas on what should be done and how. Fleeing was out of the question. For many of the species, Lake Fibian was the only home they had ever known. They wouldn't know how to survive living with other animals they did not know, even if they were the same species, nor would the truce at Lake Fibian carry over to protect them. Their lives would become a daily struggle for survival. Normal predatory species would not care who lived or died when it was time to feed.

"Maybe we can ssssqueeze them to death and ssssswallow the Hoppernotssss whole," Alina interrupted. "I bet they would have lovely crunchy bonessss. We would be rid of them forever."

"I don't think even *your* mouth is big enough to eat a Hoppernot," Mister Webster said. He appeared unaware of the insult until Alina hissed at him. "What I mean to say is you have never seen a Hoppernot before Alina. Hoppernots are too large, even for you."

Alina stretched herself over Mister Webster's squat body. He tried not to shrink away as the unmistakable flick of her forked tongue glided over the top of his head. There were too many witnesses for a snake attack, he decided. At least he hoped so.

Titus spoke up. "We need to watch them. The Hoppernots. Study their habits and discover their strengths and weaknesses. We need to get under their skin. It is the only way to defend our homes."

"We need Crissssstobel as we know for certain sssshe can understand the Hoppernotssss," Alina added.

"I don't think we need her or the other two reckless leaplings at all," Foster argued.

Notty, Cristobel's mother, shifted and spoke for the first time. "I know most of you don't trust Cristobel, Spyder or Max. I must admit, I have my doubts too, but I think . . ." She took a deep breath before saying firmly, "Let them help. Until we know differently, Cristobel is the only one who understands the Hoppernots. She will feel less afraid if Max and Spyder are with her."

Notty looked around at the solemn, worried eyes turned her way. "Cristobel is my daughter and I love her, but she must do what she can to help. She'll need help. Max is quick thinking and Spyder is more cautious. Their combined strengths will help them be successful. We don't have a choice, so let them join."

Mister Webster agreed. The other Collaboration members grudgingly conceded.

"We need to do this before everyone else returns," Foster, always the voice of reason, added. He stood to his full height and puffed out his chest, ready for battle. "If there are casualties—and I don't expect there to be—but in case there are, we need to make sure there are as few of those as possible, so we need to do this soon."

Bobbing his head, Mister Webster asked, "What do you say? Can we save Lake Fibian and be rid of the Hoppernots forever?"

He held his breath, waiting for the final verdict.

After a few moments of tense silence, Cristobel spoke up, "We are in danger and not only from the Hoppernots and their Mobilibeasts. This will be the first time we put the Collaboration Agreement to the test and we can't fail because the results will be deadly if things go wrong. We have to trust each other."

"And that twust has to start with you twusting us," Spyder added.

Mona leapt from the lake, startling everyone.

"I think I speak for the entire school of fish when I say we are ready and willing to help." Hundreds of fish leapt out of the lake – with wild frenzied flips – letting everyone know they agreed with the plan.

"I don't know what they'll be able to do," Max whispered, and then closed his mouth when Notty and Titus glared over at him.

"Well?" Titus asked the others.

Tobias, Alina, and Laramy agreed. The strength of their promise encouraged the other leaders to join in.

"So, that's it then," cried Max. "We begin to plan a battle."

"Yes," Mister Webster agreed. "Per the Collaboration Agreement, the strengths and special talents of each species have been documented. What we need to do is create a plan that uses our special skills. I propose we scout out Sprocket Point House from the sky, from the ground, and everywhere in between. Gather as much information as possible and meet back here daily to report our findings."

"We will be ssssucessssul," Alina hissed as she slithered past.

Miss Milly, who had been unusually silent during the entire discussion, spoke up. "Yes, we will be." She gripped her fingers tightly together and took a deep breath. "We have to be."

thirteen
The Box Shaped Box

Psst.

Pause.

Psssssssst.

Cristobel opened bleary eyes as an insistent sound penetrated her sleep. It had taken a long time for her eyes to close for the night; now the annoying noise was pulling her out of a pleasant dream of sitting in the shade eating sweet berries from the forbidden Prickle Berry bush.

She grumbled and looked over at the small open hollow where the noise was coming from. Two familiar faces—Max with a huge, eager smile and Spyder with a worry line between his large eyes—stared at her from between her open curtains.

She sighed. She knew what this meant. Max must have thought up some new adventure. Ordinarily she would be excited, but this time Cristobel would side with Spyder's more cautious nature.

"What are you two doing here?" she whispered.

"Come outside and we'll tell you," Max whispered back, then leaped down to the ground before Cristobel could ask more questions. Spyder held on to the edge of the hollow and bobbed his head tiredly. He looked like she felt. His large eyes haunted and ringed with an unnatural shadow. He needed more than sleep to take away the fear she saw in them.

"I'll be right down," she told him and slipped from underneath her cozy moss and pussy willow cover.

Cristobel found them sitting on a root of the large tree outside her home. It was still dark outside, but she could see evidence of the sun making its slow rise in the distance. The budding leaves diluted the small amount of light filtering down from the shifting moon, leaving her two friends hidden in the shadows. She hoped they were the only things hidden in the shadows and briefly thought about asking them to come inside the house, but knew they would awaken her mother who was a light sleeper.

Cristobel hopped down and stood next to Spyder.

"Okay, what's so important it couldn't wait until tomorrow?"

"It is tomorrow," Max chirped with a quick grin.

"You know what I mean." Cristobel was as exasperated as she was nervous. Standing out in the open, even if it was right outside her home was not a good idea when they didn't know where the Hoppernots or the Mobilibeasts were.

"When I was sitting in the tree, right before the Mobilibeast attacked Mister Fowler," Max began, "I saw something on the other side of Sprocket Point House. It was big, almost as tall as Sprocket Point House and it wasn't there before the Deep Sleep. I think we should go back and look around."

Spyder and Cristobel looked at each other skeptically.

"He's up to something," Cristobel said.

Turning to Max, she said, "Whatever it is we don't want any part of it. I want to go back to sleep."

"It might be important," Max insisted.

Spyder sighed. "I didn't see anything and I was behind the house."

"It was farther back from the house. I didn't see it until I was higher up in the tree, higher than we were the day before." Max sat back on his hind legs and somberly stared at his friends. "I think we should go back and investigate."

Spyder's throat warbled. He swallowed and raised his hand to stop his friend from saying any more.

Cristobel's jaw dropped. "I think we should wait until the leaders get together again and tell them what you saw."

"I agwee with Crithobel," Spyder added quickly.

"Look, I know you're scared. I'm scared too, but look at what we found out when we went there the first time. *We* brought information back to the Elders and *we* discovered a secret weapon against the Hoppernots."

"What secwet weapon?"

"Cristobel."

"I'm not a weapon," Cristobel croaked.

Max and Spyder looked her way, causing her discomfort to rise. She hadn't figured out how or why she was able to understand the Hoppernots, but she knew she would be questioned more thoroughly about it. She wished she had the answer.

"Look what happened to Mister Fowler," Spyder said.

At the mention of Mister Fowler's name they were silent for a moment. They hadn't heard from Doctor

Tom before the Collaboration meeting broke up the night before. His condition was unknown.

"We're going to get in trouble," Cristobel said.

"Maybe."

"If we do this without telling the Collaboration leaders they won't allow us to help."

"Highly doubtful," Max said, and then smiled wide, "especially when we come back with important information."

"Or dead," Spyder said.

"We can't do it. Not this time, Max. My mother stood up for us in front of the entire Collaboration. She got them to trust us."

"We made a pwomise and we can't bweak a pwomise," Spyder added.

"Actually," Max said with a smile, "we didn't. We said we would do everything they told us to do. They haven't told us what to do or what not to do yet, so—"

"Well, well, well," someone squawked.

The trio jumped.

"Well?" Mantu's silky voice called down from a branch above. "What are the three of you talking about?"

Max, Spyder, and Cristobel took a collective breath, relieved the intruder was a crow and not a Hoppernot. Mantu's sudden appearance was unexpected; he normally stayed closer to the lake and kept to the tops of the trees this early in the morning.

Feeling his heart slow back to its normal beat, Max opened his mouth to answer, but Mantu interrupted.

"Don't bother making something up young Max. I overheard everything you said."

"Then why did you ask?" Max grumbled.

Mantu opened his wings and glided down to the ground so that he was eye level with the three leaplings standing on the tree root. "You should listen to your friends, Max. The Collaboration would consider what you are planning to be a promise broken."

Spyder spun around to look at Max and stuck his tongue out.

"Why are you here, anyway?" Max demanded.

"I requested to stand guard on this section of the woods because I knew you three would have planned something risky," Mantu paused to let his words sink in. "While I have never been one to stop you three from enjoying your adventures—and yes, I know all about the near debacle in the redwood tree."

He looked at Spyder. "Didn't you wonder where that old empty bird's nest came from? Nicer to fall into that than all the way to the hard earth."

Spyder swallowed and lowered his eyes.

"I also know about the more recent Limmon incident." He glared over at Max, then turned his head and spoke directly to Cristobel, "And the last year's berries. But this time leaplings, I must intervene. This is not a game. The Hoppernots are to be approached with caution and strategy. You have no idea what they are capable of doing."

"And you do?" Max blurted.

"As a matter of fact, I do. I also know about the box you saw near the house, Max. I agree it needs to be looked into, but we need to discuss this with the Collaboration Leaders."

"But—"

"You must abide by the laws set forth by the Agreement. This is a time of peril and if one species works without the consent of the others, you open everyone up to discord and possible war among the species. You are young. You don't know what it's like to live your entire life in fear."

Mantu almost laughed out loud at his own words, but he finally understood the importance of the Collaboration Agreement. Meeting one's ultimate enemies put things into perspective like nothing else could.

"Mantu," Max began, "you're a member of the Collaboration, so it would be alright if we went with you to check things out."

Mantu shook his head.

"You know all they'll do is waste time talking. If we go now we can bring back information. It'll be done already."

Max grinned.

Mantu closed his eyes and sighed, then mumbled "troublemaker" under his breath.

"Come on. Let's go," Mantu commanded. He leaped into the air and circled above their heads, then led the way.

"The lake is in the other direction, Mantu," Cristobel called out.

"I know." Mantu, flying not too far above the leaplings, headed toward the box.

Astonished he was moving in the opposite direction from where the Elders could be found, they followed.

As they hopped in the direction of Sprocket Point House, Spyder asked Max, "Bewwies? I wonder what bewwies he's talking about."

Neither Spyder nor Max looked at Cristobel. She knew exactly what berries Mantu meant and it got her thinking.

fourteen
. . . In the Act

The Three were halfway to Sprocket Point House when they were stopped.

Foster, also suspicious of the trio, was on his way to check on them when he spotted Cristobel, Max, and Spyder. He wasn't surprised to see them sneaking their way toward Sprocket Point House, but he was shocked at the sight of Mantu leading the way.

"Not one word from any of you," Foster snapped, when all four opened their mouths to speak.

Foster screeched out the angry notes of the Collaboration call requesting the presence of the other leaders. In frosty silence, they waited until the others arrived.

When the bewildered animals gathered around, they listened in surprise as Foster told them what was going on.

"Why didn't you say something last night?" Foster demanded. He snapped his right wing against his body, causing a rush of air to blow over Max's face.

"Oh I'm sorry, we were just a little bit distracted." Max was tired of being yelled at by Foster, but none of the Anura Elders were sticking up for him.

Foster's black chest rose as he sucked in a breath at the insolence. Cristobel, seeing nothing but trouble heading Max's way, intervened.

"We were scared."

Foster flew over to stand in front of Mantu. "How did you get involved?"

The animals were uncomfortable. Foster's belligerence was obvious and no one, other than Mantu, wanted to confront or face down the old puffed up eagle.

Mantu ignored him and Foster harrumphed when he realized Mantu wasn't going to answer.

The crowd, not as large as the night before, included members of every animal species, the leaders of the Collaborations, their seconds in charge and the top members of their security teams. The rest of the security members were spread out around the lake making sure everyone was safe in their homes and staying calm. The last thing they needed was someone wrongfully believing they could take on the Hoppernots.

Titus stepped forward. His suspicious eyes glared at *The Three.* They squirmed. Titus stepped closer to Spyder. The black spidery lines circling Spyder's body grew more distinct as he tried to avoid Titus' eyes.

Titus pushed himself up on his hind legs and expanded his throat. His eyes bulged out of their already large sockets.

Spyder, who understood Titus' look and stance, stammered little croaks. He knew he was the weakest link between himself, Max, and Cristobel.

"I saw *The Three* on their way here," Mantu said smoothly. Stepping closer to Spyder, he looked down and winked at him.

Spyder slumped. Had Mantu not stepped forward, he would have spilled the secret of that morning's aborted mission.

"I overheard them talking about a large box by Sprocket Point House. I realized no one had mentioned seeing the structure last night. After discussing it, we realized—rightly, it would appear—that no one other than Max and I noticed it."

Max flicked his eyes toward Mantu. "Umm, yeah, I forgot. I . . . with Mister Fowler's attack and everything going on yesterday, the box slipped my mind."

"Now," Mantu continued, "I think the leaplings and I should go and check out the box."

Mantu's declaration caused an outburst of righteous indignation, which achieved his goal of shifting attention away from *The Three* and focusing it on figuring out the next steps.

"Why in the name of lightning do you think that?" Foster demanded.

"We're small," Cristobel said. "We're smaller than most of the Collaboration. We'll be easier to overlook."

"Mantu's fast," Spyder added.

"If we have too many animals approaching the Hoppernots at once," Mantu argued, "they may become violent before we are ready to defend ourselves. In this instance, less and swift is more powerful."

Heads volleyed back and forth as Mantu and Foster began to argue, but Mantu was a master strategist and a manipulator.

"I told you all they'd do is talk," Max croaked. "I wish they'd get on with it. We have an adven...uhh, a mission to do."

"We may be here all day. Once these two get going there's no shutting them up," Cristobel replied.

"I wish we could stuff their mouths with fire ants," Spyder croaked. "Then they'd have to shut up."

Spyder heard two loud *squawks* and realized Foster and Mantu had overheard him. He shrunk down closer to the ground when they glared at him.

"Why should it be you?" Foster groused. "I think we need to vote on this."

"Why not me? I happen to know the exact location of the box," Mantu replied smoothly.

"I'm faster," Foster added smugly.

"You used to be faster," Mantu interrupted. "When you were younger that is and since I am younger than you . . ."

"They're arguing again," Max grumbled. He began to hop from foot to foot.

Cristobel raised her voice, "If you two don't stop we're leaving without either of you."

"You will not, young lady," Titus yelled.

Cristobel opened her mouth to respond, then raised her hands. She shushed the animals nearest her and stared through the trees as she heard raised voices, like a wave, coming toward them from the direction of the Burrow.

If the crowd was scared before, whatever information was being passed along created a higher level of panic.

A turtle popped it head out of its shell and squeaked, "What's happening?"

"How is he?" squealed a hedgehog, who rolled itself into a tight ball and collided into the turtle. Turtle promptly tucked its head away.

Dotted throughout the trees, birds flapped their wings and squawked, repeating the same questions over and over until the squirrels began shushing everyone when one of the Golden Mantella frogs' appeared with Doctor Tom.

Doctor Tom walked ahead of him watching the sky, peering through the trees and searching through the throng. They stopped in the middle of the gathering and gravely looked around at the varying expressions among the different species.

Without any preamble, Doctor Tom announced, "Mister Fowler is in a coma."

Gasps erupted throughout the crowd and terrified shrieks pierced the air. Miss Milly, who was using her green hopping shoot to push her way through to the front of the crowd, promptly fainted into the arms of a badger.

"I guess we'll meet you back at the lake," Max said.

Both Spyder and Cristobel elbowed him in the belly.

fifteen Skulking

Spyder, Cristobel, and Max clutched hands. They'd never been high in the air before without being in a tree. They were equal parts excited and scared. Looking at Lake Fibian from the air was a once in a lifetime opportunity for the trio. They didn't want to miss a second of it.

Mantu's feathers were soft and silky, almost slippery, but the leaplings held on tight as he flew higher and higher above the tree line.

Soaring above the land and the lake, Max was speechless, Cristobel gazed around with wide unblinking eyes and Spyder was stuffing his mouth with earthworm water taffy trying not to look down.

The sun was high in the sky and the air still cool from the change of night to day. Mantu flew in tighter and tighter circles while they all surveyed the land around Sprocket Point House.

"I know you're probably scared flying this high," Mantu said, "but I need to make sure everything is safe before we land."

"I'm not scared," Max croaked, although he looked greener than usual.

As Mantu continued to glide, they scanned the trees, the house, and the grounds; their sharp eyes missed nothing. The box was a good distance away from the house and tucked under the shelter of the trees which was helpful in case the Hoppernots were inside the house, but so far, they were nowhere to be seen, nor could they hear any noises other than those made by the animals hiding in the woods.

Mantu gently landed on a tree branch above the new structure. The four of them stared at the large white rectangular box. There were four closed windows and one closed door. The box looked impenetrable, but they needed to find a way inside to see what new menace the Hoppernots brought with them.

Going inside was not the ideal plan. Mantu hoped the small frogs would find a way into the building unobserved if the Hoppernots returned. Discovering what the Hoppernots were doing, or planning to do, was imperative.

Mantu shivered and noticed the little frogs were shaking and gripping the branch. He could not tell if it was because of the flight, their closeness to the Hoppernots or both, but their terror was obvious in the rapid blinking of their eyes and quick, labored breathing. He gazed down at them until each one looked up and nodded.

"Wh-what do we do now?" Spyder asked.

"We need to get inside of that thing," Mantu replied, staring intently at the large box. "How in the world did they get a structure this size in the middle of our woods without anyone noticing?"

Mantu began to pace back and forth. He opened and closed his beak over and over again with a loud snap.

"This is a serious threat and no one noticed it," he grumbled. He stopped pacing and breathed air into his beak.

"How are we going to get in?" Max asked. For the first time during an adventure, his mind was completely blank.

"It doesn't look like there's a way for us to get in," Cristobel added.

"I'll fly down and take a closer look," Mantu volunteered.

"You can't go down there alone," Cristobel said, horrified at the idea of being so close to the Hoppernots again.

"Did any of you see the Mobilibeasts?" she asked.

"No, but maybe they left and won't return," Max said hopefully.

"Or," Spyder whimpered, "maybe they're stealthy and hiding, waiting for us to make a mistake before they attack us."

"They're not here," Mantu said. "They're large enough that I would have seen something unusual when we flew over here, but I will make a quick fly close to the ground to see if I can find them and then I will investigate the box."

"How does he know what they look like?" Max whispered as Mantu leapt from the branch and began a fast and silent glide toward the ground and through the trees.

Max kept quiet after that, as did his companions. They tried to keep their eyes on Mantu as he flew. They held their breaths until Mantu sent out a quiet *caw-caw* to let them know he was safe when he was out of their sight.

Cristobel gripped the boys' hands as Mantu neared the box below their perch. They did not move, nor did they make a sound as they watched him glide above the box a few times, and then lower to circle its perimeter. Their eyes darted around. They listened intently to make sure they were still alone.

There were no Hoppernot voices, or any sound of a returning Mobilibeast.

They let their collectively held breath go when Mantu returned. Cristobel was so happy he returned unscathed, she released her friends' hands, hopped over to Mantu and hugged his leg. Mantu was startled, but he didn't say anything to her. He too was glad to be safe.

"The only oddity I saw," Mantu said, "was some strange impressions with lines and ridges of various sizes on the ground. They were around the box and leading to and from Sprocket Point House and down the new path. Other than that, we appear to be alone. The Mobilibeasts are not here, nor do I see the Hoppernots. As for the box, it looks completely sealed."

"I wonder what it is?" Spyder mused. "Why would the Hoppewnots keep a box that didn't do anything? Doesn't make sense."

"Why don't you take us down there Mantu?" Max asked. "Maybe we'll see something you missed."

Mantu raised a black brow at the leapling, but said nothing. He needed time to think.

"Come on," Max pleaded. "Let's go already."

"I don't want to take you any closer to it," Mantu sighed, and then lightly tapped his beak together. "But we need to find out its secrets. It's highly doubtful the Hoppernots would bring a big box like this to the middle of the woods for no reason."

"As much as I want to disagwee with Max, I don't think we have a choice." Spyder added and silently wished he had another piece of taffy. He concentrated better when he ate.

"It could be a trap," Mantu mumbled. "We could get caught in a trap I haven't seen or those sneaky creatures could be planning another sneak attack."

Mantu looked over at the leaplings who watched him with large, worried eyes. "We can't do this," he insisted. "Hoppernots are wily creatures. One of you could get hurt, or worse, killed."

Tipping his head to the side, Sprocket Point House caught his eye. He groaned and turned his back to it.

Snapping his wings against his sides, Mantu argued, "The whole point of flying out here was to investigate even if it means risking our lives."

"What's he going on about?" Max asked.

"No idea," Spyder answered.

Mantu cleared his throat and declared, "There is no other way." He walked toward the leaplings and said, "Climb on up."

Mantu flew around the box, circling and looking, circling and looking. He needed to make sure he took all precautions before he put their lives in danger. The last thing he wanted to do was return to the lake and tell the Collaboration Leaders that one of the leaplings was injured or killed under his watch. So, he flew around awhile until he heard Max say, "Any time now."

Mantu grumbled under his breath, but could no longer stall. With one final pass around the box, he landed on top of it.

Cristobel, Max, and Spyder leaped off his back, each facing a different direction, making sure they were alone.

"I think we're safe," Cristobel whispered.

"Let's look around and see if there are any cracks we can slip into," Max suggested.

The trio hopped in the directions they were facing. No one spoke as they looked around the heated top of the box. Mantu stood still, moving only his head to search the area.

No new sights or sounds came from the woods.

"I . . . I think I found something," Spyder called out. His voice was low and wobbly. He heard a quiet noise come from beneath his feet, but when he turned to look at his friends, they seemed intent on their own search and didn't hear the sound.

"What is it?" Max hopped over to Spyder's side.

"What's that noise?" Cristobel asked when she joined them, not having found a way in.

Mantu shushed them. He leaned over and laid his head next to the protruding square object Spyder found. It was the same color as the roof and easy to miss from the sky. He noticed a small space and eyed the trio next to him, sizing them up.

"I think you'll fit," he said abruptly.

"Fit what?" Spyder asked.

"Fit where?" Max chimed in.

Laying her body flat, Cristobel was able to see the space Mantu pointed at with his beak. "Maybe," she agreed, "but it might be a little tight. I wonder where it leads."

"The only way to find out is to squeeze through and go in," Mantu replied, then looked over at Spyder. "Hmm, I don't know if you'll be able to make it. You're pretty plump for your size."

Spyder pushed himself up to his hind legs and sucked in his belly. Okay, he was a little bigger than the average leapling, but he certainly knew how to make himself small enough to squeeze into a tight place.

"I'm going with them," he said.

"Of course you are Spy," Cristobel said soothingly. Although she too wondered if her friend could fit into the small space.

"I'll even go first."

And he did. He squeezed his little round body into the small tight space and was almost through when his rump got stuck.

Rolling his eyes, Max raised his webbed foot, laid it against Spyder's backside and pushed.

They heard a muffled yelp, and then Spyder's voice called out, "I'm okay, I'm okay. Uhh…" There was a pause and then they heard a smacking sound. In a muffled voice Spyder said, "I think it's safe to come in."

"Is he eating?" Mantu asked incredulous.

"I wouldn't be surprised," Cristobel answered.

Turning to Max and Cristobel, Mantu warned, "Now hurry back and don't take any chances. Memorize everything you see and hear, but most importantly pay attention. If you are in trouble I want you to *chirp-trill-chirp-chirp-croak* to let me know."

"Then what?" Max asked. "This is the only way in and you're too big to fit."

"I don't know, but I hope I don't have to figure that out. Now go and remember to be careful."

Mantu watched as Max and Cristobel squatted and squeezed their way into the darkness of the box. He stood outside as the sun rose higher in the sky.

Alone.

sixteen
A Box is Just a Box

Spyder's eyes narrowed when Max and Cristobel entered the dark tunnel.

"What's wrong?" she asked.

"What took you so long? I've been down here for an owa."

"It wasn't an hour. It was only a minute. Don't be a scaredy, Spy. We'll be fine," Max replied.

"You always say that when we're about to get into twouble."

"Not now guys." Cristobel looked down the tunnel, which wasn't very long. A single strip of sunlight filtered into the crack they came in through and showed several openings at the bottom of the tunnel.

At the far end was an object that looked like a twisted four-leaf clover. Max, thinking it was a hairy plant-like object, was surprised when he jumped on a hard, dust-filled surface. He had to grip tight to its edges as it turned in fast circles. It made a whop-whop-whop sound as it turned and Max could feel the whip of the air as it continued its mad spin.

The edges were thin and sharp like the edge of the rock-blades they used to cut down Stink-Shrooms that popped up in the middle of summer. The sharpness of the blade hurt Max's fingers and toes.

Max did not croak, chirp or scream. He wanted to, but he didn't because he did not want to alert their enemies to their presence.

After a minute or two, the four-leaf clover or blade or whatever it was began to slow down. When he could, Max put his leg out toward the wall and gripped it with his spread toes. When he stopped moving Max gulped as the contents of his stomach rumble a protest.

"What is going on down there? Are you okay?" Mantu's muffled voice floated down to them.

Cristobel, not wanting to worry the crow, said, "Yes, we're fine. We're, uh, getting our bearings. We're about to go further down." She couldn't hear what he said, but she assumed Mantu grunted.

"What is that thing?" Spyder asked, staring at the faux four-leaf clover skeptically. Max was safe, but that didn't mean the thing he stood on wasn't dangerous.

Max rubbed his stomach, then ran his fingers over his face. His hand was shaking, but it was too late to change course.

"I don't know what it is, but it moves at the slightest touch and the edges are sharp, so be careful. Why don't you two jump over it and slip in through the opening on the other side? I'll hold it steady and follow behind once you get through. Umm, Cristobel, why don't you go in first and look around?"

Cristobel and Spyder knew the reason behind Max's suggestion. When Spyder was overcome with fear, especially if he was alone, he croaked uncontrollably and hopped in place erratically or he became mute and froze in place. How he made it through the crack without cracking up, they'd never know, but they didn't want to take any more chances.

Cristobel slipped through the cold, silver slats and quietly croaked once letting the other two know it was safe to join her. When Max appeared and hopped next to Spyder, they stood huddled on the ceiling of a room that looked similar to one of the rooms in Sprocket

Point House. A room the animals had named a water-closet, but this room was smaller and not as pleasant.

There were no cobwebs or nests on the walls or floors. They did recognize a tall white stand with a shiny silvery basin that could hold water. Next to it was a white squat bowl already filled with water. It had a mysterious silver handle that they had seen before: if pressed down, it would agitate the water inside the bowl and make the water—and any unsuspecting animal—disappear.

In the corner was a smaller room with a nearly transparent door where water fell from an apparatus close to the ceiling and into a big white dish on the floor. Unlike the room at Sprocket Point House, there were no windows to look outside, but there was a door that was cracked open enough for them to look into the next room.

They took a few giant leaps and clung to the doorframe leading into a long, large single room. It was semi-dark inside except for a few small balls of light on the lower sections of the wall that highlighted a walkway cluttered with soft and hard looking objects the trio had never seen before.

Max took a step back, reached over Spyder's back and poked Cristobel. He pointed a shaky finger toward one of the objects on the floor that looked like a large, flat duckbill. It was a different color than the one he saw on the head of the Hoppernot the day before.

Cristobel raised a trembling finger to her mouth. Spyder hadn't noticed the duckbill and she didn't want to alarm him. He would not handle this new discovery well and probably get them caught if they were discovered. She hoped he didn't notice it.

They continued to look around, making sure the area was safe. They saw a number of objects with four wooden legs, a flat surface holding them together and an intricate wooden back. To the left of the water-closet were a couple of large rough covered objects, similar to what used to be in Sprocket Point House that the original Hoppernot used to sit or lie on.

To the right, beyond the covered walls, the area was shadowed, but the trio could see a tall, silvery box, next to a long flat surface area –one side was white and had four black strange circular knobs in front and four dark spirals on top. The other side looked like a dull silver tub with two glass knobs and a long silver stem hovering over the top. They could hear the steady *plop* and *ping* of dripping water.

A whirring sound came from the back of the big box and a blast of cold air, similar to, though sharper than, the kind of cold that came during winter months, touched their skin. It was an eerie feeling, unnatural in its bite.

To warm up, Cristobel thought of the warmth of the sun and Spyder thought of hot pot pepper stew. Spyder looked over at Max who didn't seem to notice. He was staring at the walls. Spyder looked closer at them and then stared as intently as Max.

No, not walls. At least not solid ones. It looked like there was something soft covering the walls that moved along with the cold air passage on both sides of the room. Some type of thick material fell from ceiling to floor.

One of the long sheets billowed out uncovering what was hidden beneath - not a covered wall, but what looked like long, darkened alcoves.

"Let's get closer and see what's under there," Max whispered. He took a giant leap, then stopped. He flipped around to make sure Spyder and Cristobel followed.

"Let's start with the nearest ones," Cristobel suggested. They were closest to their escape route.

"Okay, I'll look in the top and middle ones. Cristobel, you take the lower one and Spyder . . ." Max could see the terrified look on Spyder's face and knew he wouldn't be insulted when he said, "You be the look out, just in case."

"Just in case of what?" Spyder squawked, although he was relieved. The box was empty so there was little cause of concern for a "just in case" occurrence. He hoped.

Neither Max nor Cristobel answered. They hopped over to the edge of the wall. Max slipped through the opening on top and Cristobel pushed aside the billowing curtain and entered the bottom alcove.

Max jumped inside the alcove and landed on something fur-like. He was standing on the top of a round dome, clutching fur that was thin and slippery, even more slippery than Mantu's feathers. At first he was afraid, but then he thought maybe one of the other animals had seen the big box too and came in to investigate.

"Who is it?" Max asked, but received no response. "It's me. Max of the Anura. Who are you?"

Still no response. Max was about to move when the animal spoke. It was a weird sound, kind of like a growling-croaking-snort, but he didn't understand what the animal meant, nor did he know who or what he was dealing with. He shrunk in on himself, becoming smaller. His nerves tightened and twitched.

What if the Hoppernots brought another kind of beast into the woods with them? Just because no one had seen anything other than the Hoppernots and the Mobilibeasts in the area did not mean the Hoppernots didn't bring other equally dangerous beasts with them.

The longer he stayed in the darkened alcove with an animal who refused to identify itself, the higher his fear rose. Max was about to hop to the left and leave the enclosure, but before he could move, a loud, blaring sound unlike anything he had ever heard before exploded through the quiet of the outer room. He hopped backward, turning his body and landing on the wall behind him, then covered his ears. He couldn't seem to think and he couldn't move. The noise paralyzed his muscles. The swift tide of terror coursing through his blood wasn't helping matters at all.

Cristobel's eyes quickly adjusted to the darkness. She heard a guttural noise that sounded like a sleeping bear. She landed on a soft surface that almost swallowed her whole. She let out a quick chirp when a sharp object poked her belly. Leaping away, she saw the end of a feather sticking out from the place she'd landed. A feather? Maybe it was some kind of nest. Did the Hoppernots plan to keep captured birds, she wondered?

The noise sounded again and then a large, pale appendage—a paw or a hand—flopped down next to her throwing her so high in the air she had to rotate her body, stretch out her arms and legs and hope her toes connected to a surface she could stick to. With a *thwack* she landed on the ceiling of the alcove and had a bird's eye view of . . .

Not an alcove.

It took everything inside of Cristobel not to trill out the loudest, longest croak of her life, but she managed to stop. She closed her eyes and wished like she never wished before that she was in the middle of a horrible nightmare and all she needed to do was have her mother wake her up, stroke her brow and give her white birch tea to sooth her back to sleep.

She opened her eyes. All the hope in her died as she watched the pale body of a real life Hoppernot sleeping noisily below her. The growls had grown louder when it turned over and now sounded ferocious. She heard the creature take a deep breath and watched as its chest expanded and deflated, then slowly move up and down, barely moving as if to confuse its enemy into thinking it was dead.

She needed to get out of the sleeping chamber, return to her friends and get out of there. She took one step preparing to leap as close to the opening as she could when a noise unlike any other almost scared the yellow off of her.

For the second time in Spyder's life he was not thinking about food. Not eating it. Not smelling it. Not anticipating it. He was so scared his usual voracious hunger was nonexistent and he feared he would never be hungry again. Worst of all his right leg was trembling. He had to tap his foot to shake the nerves causing his leg to twitch uncontrollably. He feared the thumping noise would distract his friends and cause them to make a mistake.

Spyder drew in a deep breath as he watched Cristobel and Max disappear behind the curtains and into the darkened alcoves. He was vulnerable. Not only was he sitting alone in a strange box, baffled about the purpose of the box, but he watched his best friends enter the alcoves with anxiety. Neither he, nor they, had any weapons to protect themselves.

Sure, he could make noise and sound alarms calling for help, but he didn't know if he would be heard outside the box. If the old stories about the Hoppernot were true, one of them could be hiding this very minute and could attack them so fast he would not be able to get out a single croak to warn Mantu.

He looked around one more time, easing his mind that he was alone. Spyder hopped closer to the door that lead back to the exit where Mantu waited. He wanted to make sure nothing and no one would come to any harm on his watch.

He was in mid-leap and almost to the door, when a blast of sound startled him. He lost his concentration and then his footing.

Spyder plummeted to the ground.

seventeen
Hide and (Reluctantly) Seek

Cristobel peeked out from behind the curtain. Her eyes were glued to the legs covered with dark curling fur. They kicked out from behind the curtain on the opposite side of the alcove where she and Max were hidden. The Hoppernot stood up to its full height and stretched its long arms above its head, then bent its back as far as it would go until a quick succession of pops sounded. Straightening, the Hoppernot scratched its underbelly, then its face.

A loud grunt and groan sounded from the bunk Max hid behind.

"Turn off the alarm already," a gruff voice called out.

"I'm working on it," said the standing Hoppernot.

"How about working on some coffee while you're at it," said gruff-voiced Hoppernot.

"I'm going to stop being a morning person," it grumbled. "I seem to be doing all the work."

Cristobel watched until the standing Hoppernot was nothing but a shadow on the far end of the room. The other Hoppernot voices, still hidden within the sleeping chambers, quieted down.

The Hoppernot enclosed with Cristobel sat up when a warm dark smell of percolating mist floated around the room. She did not move and was relieved that when she'd jumped she landed in a darkened section where the Hoppernot was unable to see her. At least she hoped it could not.

Turning her body so that she could keep an eye on both Hoppernots, she was about to sneak away when she heard a heavy gurgling sound. It came from the Hoppernot's throat. She watched in alarm as the Hoppernot turned its head and stared straight at her.

The Hoppernot inhaled sharply, opened its eyes wide and shouted "*Achoo*" at her and then said, "*Whattha . . .*" as it tried to reach for her.

She didn't understand what the words meant, but she knew it was time to leave.

Cristobel scrambled out of the enclosure and immediately saw that Spyder was not too far away but was much lower to the ground than the last time she saw him.

Spyder was hopping as fast as his chubby body allowed. She took a long leap and plopped next to him, startling him so badly he lost his grip, but as he was falling he grabbed on to a hard protruding nub sticking out of the wall. As soon as his grip firmed, stopping him from falling, the nub began to move down, lighting up the room and forcing Spyder to take a deep breath and hurl himself as far as he could go. With a couple of wobbly hops, he landed next to Cristobel near the top portion of the door, close to their escape route through the ceiling of the water-closet.

Holding on to his belly and trying to catch his breath Spyder asked, "Where's Max?"

Cristobel stopped moving and turned her body around to look back toward the covered sleeping chambers.

No Max.

"I don't know," she replied.

"We can't leave him. What should we do?"

"We have to call him. I know it's dangerous, but we can't leave without him."

Spyder took a deep breath. His throat expanded farther than it ever had and he let out the longest, loudest croak of his life.

The entire room went silent.

The Hoppernots stopped their grunted conversations and the one in the top bunk where Max was hidden yelped.

The Hoppernot leaped out from behind the curtain. Its arms tangled in the fabric causing it to rip from the clips holding it up as they both fell to the ground.

"Something touched me," yelled the Hoppernot.

The Hoppernot thrashed around, waving its arms and kicking its legs wildly. "Whatever it is, kill it."

"What is it?" another Hoppernot asked.

"Something slimy that jumps. I don't know what it is but kill it if you see it."

Spyder croaked again, louder this time, desperate to see Max.

"Hurry Max," Cristobel called out.

A loud answering croak sounded and Max leaped toward the open door.

"Go-go-go-go-go!" Max yelled and his friends moved toward the opening in the ceiling of the bathroom without hesitation.

"What about the four-leaf clover?" Cristobel asked as they drew near the opening.

"It's not moving. Quick, let's get through it," Spyder replied.

All three squeezed pass the hard leaves including Max who made it through the tight exit in record time as one of the Hoppernots touched something on the wall, which flooded the water-closet with light and made the four-leaf clover start to spin again.

As Cristobel pulled her feet through the exit on top, she heard the muffled sound of the Hoppernots talking.

The Hoppernot in the water-closet started yelling, while the others laughed. By the sounds the Hoppernots made, Cristobel understood they were amused.

"What was that thing?" The Hoppernot who had worn the duckbill the day before asked. "It touched me. I think it bit me."

"It was just a frog. A tiny frog can't hurt a tough man like you," another Hoppernot teased. "Stop being such a scaredy-cat."

"Mantu, you should have seen them," Max exclaimed. "They were terrified of us."

"Tell me everything once we land," Mantu replied.

The flight back to the lakefront was swift. So swift, the only one who didn't get queasy was Mantu. As they escaped through the trees, Mantu, who still did not know what had happened inside the box, waited to ask them about it. The speed with which *The Three* left the opening in the roof, and Max's constant croaking of "go-go-go-go-go" prevented him from peppering them with questions.

Dodging through newly opened leaves and still bare branches, Mantu felt the tight grip of the leaplings' fingers clutching his feathers. He couldn't tell if they were holding on so tightly because of the speed or if something had happened to them, but Mantu was sure he felt a little sticky substance – compliments of Spyder's stomach – matting the feathers behind his neck. When he slowed down and gently landed on the soft grass covered ground, Mantu heard their collective sighs of relief.

Max and Cristobel leaped off Mantu's back and onto unsteady legs. Spyder, feeling woozy, rolled down the crow's body and collapsed in a heap at Mantu's clawed feet.

Mantu looked down at Spyder and, in an uncharacteristic move, stroked Spyder's back with the tip of his wing until he heard Spyder say, "I'm alwight, but I got a little sick on your back."

Miss Milly hopped forward with cups of Chipmunk Delight hoping the drink would revive the leaplings. Mantu looked on as Cristobel, Max, and Spyder greedily drank down the liquid. He wished he could partake of the sweet sticky drink because his nerves were jangled, but he had to wait until he got home. The last thing he wanted to do was show the Collaboration Leaders how rattled he was.

Doctor Tom pushed through the gathering crowd to see Cristobel, Max, and Spyder for himself.

"How is Mister Fowler?" Cristobel asked, anxiously.

"He's still in a comatose state. My senior students are watching over him." When more questions were asked, Doctor Tom raised his hands and said, "All we can do is make him comfortable and wait it out. There's nothing else to say."

He hopped over to *The Three.*

"Cristobel, you look fine," he proclaimed. "Spyder your coloring's paler than usual. A couple glasses of Chipmunk Delight and you'll be right as a thunder storm."

Miss Milly stepped closer with the tray of Chipmunk Delight. Doctor Tom handed the acorn shells filled with the drink and watched Spyder a few seconds longer as he slurped down the drink. He was pleased to see Spyder's color return as he got to the bottom of his cup.

Doctor Tom turned and watched as Max awkwardly moved his cup from hand to hand and noticed a smear of bright red droplets on the back of his fingers.

"What happened to you young man?"

Max almost dropped his drink, but glanced down to where Doctor Tom was staring. "Uh, I must have cut myself, but I'm—"

"Come here," Doctor Tom demanded. He quickly opened his bag, pulled out a blue hollowed out pebble and a dandelion puff. He soaked the puff with the Stink-Shroom tincture. The Stink-Shroom smelled awful, but the thick liquid inside its stem healed cuts and scrapes.

"Oww," Max howled and tried to move away. "It stings like an angry wasp."

"True, but it'll make you feel better," Doctor Tom said calmly.

While Doctor Tom patched up Max, the rest of the crowd grew impatient.

"What happened?" Mister Webster asked. His hands were so tightly clasped they looked knotted.

"Yessss, tell ussss," Alina implored. She hung down from a branch above the gathering. The tip of her bright green tail rapped tightly around the thick branch as her head and body hung suspended. Her forked tongue flicked impatiently, trying to taste the information from the air.

"The box is not just box." Max told the crowd how they entered the box and described all they saw inside. "The box is the Hoppernots' sleeping chamber."

"A sleeping chamber? Does that mean they live here now?" Titus had pushed his bulk through the crowd of animals to stand near *The Three.*

"That's what it looks like," Cristobel answered.

"It was howwible," Spyder whispered.

"Then there was a sound," Max added, remembering what almost got them caught. "It was some kind of alarm. I think it was warning them we were there."

"That tewwible sound woke them all up and sca-wed us so bad we barely escaped with our lives." Spyder slumped down so low his head touched the ground. He covered his ears as if he could still hear the shrill, ringing sound.

Mister Webster and Miss Milly hopped closer and laid their hands on his brow and back.

Mister Webster straightened, then asked Cristobel. "What did they say?"

"Nothing much," Cristobel said. "Once the Hoppernots woke up they all started talking at once and I was too scared to try to listen to them. I'm sorry."

"No need to be sorry. You're safe and that is the most important thing," Miss Milly said.

"Max, were you able to understand the Hoppernots?" Titus asked. "How about you Spyder?"

"We didn't understand them at all," Spyder answered for them both.

Mantu noticed the eyes of every species present shift to him.

"I was too big to enter the box, and I couldn't hear what was going on inside. However, I'm sure I won't be able to understand the Hoppernot language either."

Before anyone thought to question his last statement, Tobias spoke up. "What did they smell like?"

"I wonder what they tassste like?" Alina said.

Max scrunched his face and said, "How they smelled or what they tasted like was the last thing on our minds."

"I didn't even think about how they tasted, but now that you mention it," Spyder mused and licked his wide mouth, "they're definitely not edible like flies or mosquitos."

"These are odd questions to be having at a time like this," Mister Webster grumbled.

Mantu leaped to a higher perch to eye the lake's inhabitants. He flapped his wings, tipped back his head and sent out a long, loud *cawwww* to grab everyone's attention.

When he spoke, his voice sounded hushed and urgent, but every single animal heard him.

"We were lulled into feeling safe because the first Hoppernot left and never returned. We told the young ones of all species to be careful and mindful of what they did and where they went. Each species created its own lores to ensure we remembered what happened when the first Hoppernot was here and yet, we elders—the chosen Leaders who should know better—did not heed our own advice."

"We've put everyone in danger," Miss Milly said. Her large black eyes filled with tears.

Mister Webster leaned over to a low plant and pulled out a thin furry leaf. He folded it in half and handed her the leaferchief to mop at her cheeks.

"Now, now, Miss Milly. We couldn't continue to live as we had been when the Hoppernot was here. It was inevitable we would lower our guard after so much time had past."

Mister Webster's soothing words didn't soothe her at all.

"While I am loathe to agree with Mantu, he is correct," Foster grudgingly admitted.

"It's no use casting blame," said Titus. "We can't change what has happened, but we can plan and be vigilant now."

"We need to watch them," Foster said.

"No," Max exclaimed, "We need to stop watching them."

"And start getting rid of them," Cristobel added.

"Even I agwee with that," Spyder said.

"Yes, we do," Titus agreed. "We must discover all their weaknesses and use them to our advantage. Every one of us has talents. It does not matter how big or small we are. We can defeat the Hoppernots."

"No," Mister Webster interrupted. With squinted eyes he sat back on his hind legs and in a strong, raised voice said, "We *must* defeat them."

eighteen
The Watchers

Trouble.

Deep trouble. That's what Lake Fibian and all of its inhabitants were in.

Over the next few weeks, and as each day passed, the magnitude of trying to rid Lake Fibian of its invaders overwhelmed the animals.

In the beginning of their spy missions, the Collaboration Leaders believed it would only take a few days to figure out the Hoppernots' weaknesses. But as the days passed they realized it was a monumental task.

Crows and eagles spread throughout Lake Fibian watching and reporting back to the Collaboration Leaders as more and more Hoppernots arrived. The Hoppernots came and went all day long, starting before the sun rose and leaving before it fully set for the night. Along with these new Hoppernots, came other, stranger kinds of Mobilibeasts.

These Mobilibeasts were unnatural monstrosities. They were larger, louder and longer than the first ones that had arrived and seemed to carry fewer Hoppernots in their ears.

The new Mobilibeasts were different; the Hoppernots were able to pull all sorts of odd objects out of the Mobilibeasts' ears and rumps. Sometimes a few of the Hoppernots would gather together and disappear inside the rear end of a Mobilibeast, then reappear moments later, carrying out large covered objects they would take into Sprocket Point House. None of these items ever came back out.

The Mobilibeasts never seemed to mind. They appeared to be deeply influenced by the Hoppernots as they too came and left with them each day and night. The other Hoppernots, the original ten, entered and exited the sleeping chamber throughout the day.

There were no further attacks.

The animals stationed near Sprocket Point House watched in fascination as the Hoppernots took these strange and weird gadgets from the bodies of different Mobilibeasts.

New types of sounds rang out from the house and were loud enough to scare the squirrels and birds away, but they swallowed their fears and stayed.

A sliver of moon showed through the clouds as the animals congregated on the farthest side of the Lake Fibian, far away from Sprocket Point House.

Before the next part of their mission began, Cristobel, Spyder, and Max—after many hushed conversations—came up with a theory. A theory so good that even Foster agreed with them.

"Every species has a predator who wants to dominate them," Cristobel began.

"Which is why we have the Collabowation Agweement," Spyder added.

"The key to taking Lake Fibian back is to find out what scares the Hoppernots," said Max.

"Once we do that," Cristobel concluded, "the Hoppernots and their Mobilibeasts can be driven away from our homes."

"We can contwol them," Spyder chirped.

The specialized warriors from each species would carefully approach the Hoppernots and, with soldier-like positioning, show their war moves, and hopefully, terrify them.

"With the exception of the one with the duckbill, they are not afraid of frogs," Titus spoke up. He was quite disgruntled by this discovery.

"They hardly notice most of the birds," Mantu said. "Although, a few of them got a bit nervous when Broad-winged Hawks or vultures showed some aggressiveness."

"Perhaps the larger birds of prey can be our first line of weaponry," Laramy added.

"The Hoppernotssss are terrified of snakessss," Alina said. She stretched her mouth wide baring her fangs into a frightening smile.

"They're not fond of mice," said Cristobel. "Although one of the Hoppernots did try to kill one. It got away, though."

"They keep far away from skunks," Spyder added. "I don't think they like the way they smell."

"They completely ignore Gray Squirrels and turtles," Max said.

"They've killed a couple of spiders from the Huntsman species," Mister Webster added, which quieted the group. It was an unexpected blow to all their careful planning.

After a moment, the voices of other species called out their discoveries. Titus, with his small dried out piece of bark with soft black tip and a thin piece of white birth, scribbled the information down.

Before the gathering was dismissed for the night, Cristobel told everyone to be on guard. "The Hoppernots keep talking about "Pee-ple." Some of them point at groups of Hoppernots and use the word "Pee-ple," but they all look the same as Hoppernots."

She lifted her hand, palms upward and said, "There must be Pee-ple among them, but I can't figure out who or what they are. They all look the same to me."

Titus stepped forward. "Is there anyone else who understands the Hoppernots?" he asked. "Anyone?"

Cristobel was still the only one.

The following days went by quickly. Anxiety was high and everyone was tired. The slightest sounds had the animals moving fast, but awkwardly, resulting in a few minor injuries. Doctor Tom, as well as doctors of the other species, was forced to enlist the aid of their students with all the new patients they were seeing.

At the end of a long day, Cristobel, Max, and Spyder huddled under a drooping elephant ear plant outside of Max's house. They watched as their parents and grandparents discussed the day's mission and expressing, once again, their concern of *The Three's* involvement.

Max and Cristobel felt the fatigue dragging at their eyelids, but the excitement of being involved in the planning and spying on the Hoppernots did not make them give in to their bodies need for sleep.

Max said in glee, "We are in the middle of creating a Croaklore that will be told for generations. It will be the greatest Croaklore every told!"

He tiredly punched the air and laughed. Cristobel laughed.

They sounded hysterical to Spyder's ears. He figured the lack of sleep was starting to affect them, but they didn't seem to care.

Spyder was more interested in a snooze and less enthused by the idea of more skulking and, worst of all, flying on Mantu's back again, but he grudgingly admitted he would give up a full plate of daffodil cakes to be in a Croaklore.

"Our vewy own Cwoaklore, huh?" He said drowsily and promptly fell asleep.

On an early evening in the third week of the watch, Cristobel, Max, and Spyder stood by a log, taking a much-needed break. They were waiting for Titus, Mister Webster, and the other Collaboration

Leaders to arrive with their daily observations and suggestions, when two Hoppernots appeared.

It was the first time any of the Hoppernots had come down to the lakefront since they arrived and the trio knew nothing good could come of the Hoppernots' presence so close to their homes.

They watched as the duckbilled Hoppernot and the porcupine-headed one chatted loudly as they walked toward the lake where hundreds of fish were jumping out of the water.

Max and Cristobel debated which one of them would get close enough to observe them. Spyder scrunched his body as close to the ground as he could get and sucked intently on a fly-pop. He ignored the debate and mumbled, "I'm not going any closer."

The porcupine-headed Hoppernot carried a large sack over its shoulder, while the other one held two long sticks with longer strings dangling down its back. Their raised, laughing voices put the animals throughout the woods on alert.

Bertus, one of the Blue Heron siege, was scouting the area above the lake and shrieked out a warning call to the fish when he noticed the approaching Hoppernots. Bertus was so startled to see them approaching the lake that he forgot to use the Code Hoppernot alarm call. Nonetheless, the fish and the other animals looking for places to hide understood that there was some kind of trouble and went on the alert.

The larger fish swam around and herded the small fry out of harm's way. They hastily swam deeper into the water and farther away from the shore making sure all of the little fish were guarded.

When the Hoppernots neared the water's edge, they laid down the sack and poles on the ground, then took a seat, quickly removing their foot coverings.

Cristobel, Max, and Spyder made themselves smaller by huddling close to the ground and wiggling under a cluster of mushrooms with big white caps.

When the Hoppernots spoke, Cristobel inched closer.

"Chase, I'm glad we're able to take a break away from the construction site," the duckbill-headed Hoppernot said.

"Fixing up that old house is sweaty work. I've been looking forward to snagging some fish since we got here. Do you think we'll catch some big ones, Hunter?"

"Chase and Hunter," Cristobel whispered.

"What?" Max whispered back.

"They call the one with the porcupine-head Chase. Shhh. Never mind." She took another step closer, still hidden under the mushroom.

"The construction's taking longer than planned," the duckbill–headed Hoppernot said. "The new owners are real particular on making the house as ecologically friendly as possible."

"No more shop talk. It's time to get our fishing on."

After an hour, the two Hoppernots stood with pant legs rolled up thigh high in the cold, still water.

"What happened to all the fish?" The one called Hunter asked. It scratched the top of its spiky hair, as though bewildered by the sudden absence of fish when there were so many leaping and flipping out of the lake less than an hour before.

The two Hoppernots stood in the water, their faces scrunched up as they stared out at the still water. Cristobel could hear them debating about returning to the house since "nothing was biting."

"I'm going to follow them," Max announced.

"Why don't you stay here with Spyder and I'll go," Cristobel said.

"It should be me," Max exclaimed, "I'm faster."'

"You're not that much faster," Cristobel argued. "And you make too much noise. They're bound to hear you."

"The Hoppernots are out in the open. I can blend in with the trees," Max said, "While you would—"

She and Max were still arguing, when they heard the shocked gasps of the birds and chipmunks hidden in the trees above them; Mona was swimming closer and closer to the Hoppernots.

Spyder sat up and dropped his fly-pop as he held his breath at Mona's act of defiance.

The Hoppernots stopped talking and watched as a line of bubbles headed their way. They stood as still as tree trunks and fixed their eyes on the lone fish.

They tightened their hands on the wooden poles and waited.

The entire community of animal species held its collective breath as the rogue fish approach the motionless Hoppernots.

"It's Mona," someone hidden in a tree murmured. Startled gasps rippled around the lake.

"What is she doing?" asked a member of Mona's school.

Helpless, the animals watched as Mona defiantly swam faster and faster toward her nemeses. Taking a deep breath she leapt into the air and landed in the water with a loud and impressive splash, throwing water on the unsuspecting interlopers.

Bewildered, the Hoppernots turned and sprinted toward the shore, spluttering and wiping the water off their faces.

"What was that about?" the porcupine-head asked.

"I have no idea," the other Hoppernot replied. "All I know is that I can't wait until . . . Ahhhhhhh!"

It screamed and sprinted into the woods. It did not look back.

Without another thought, Cristobel shot forward. She jumped into an opening on the side of the sack the Hoppernot had dropped on the ground. She held her breath and held on tight as she waited.

Porcupine-head watched the other Hoppernot run into the woods, heading to Sprocket Point House. It turned around to see what made its friend move so fast. Without a sound, the Hoppernot grabbed its sack from the ground and ran.

Squeezing her eyes shut, Cristobel bounced from side to side inside the rough material. Taking a deep breath, she forced her eyes open and spied a long piece of string hanging down. She tried to grab hold of it but every time her hand drew near it, she was thrown to the other side or flopped down to the bottom of the sack and tossed back up in the air. Strange items she'd never seen before struck her body again and again. She barely got a glimpse of the foreign objects when she bit her tongue and forced herself not to squeal in pain.

Cristobel could feel her heart beat, normally a nice slow bump inside her chest, but now it raced like a jackrabbit across a field.

She grabbed onto the string. "Finally," she huffed out, but no sooner had her fingers curled around it, she smacked her head against a hard square object that bounced up from the bottom of the sack. She knew she would get a few bruises later. Belatedly, it entered her mind that she may get in big trouble with the Collaboration, and even more trouble with her parents and the Elders, for doing something so dangerous, but it would be worth it if she brought back useful information.

She pushed her face through the opening of the rough fabric and peeked out. She listened closely as the Hoppernots' spoke.

"Did a rabid squirrel chase you through the woods or are you pretending you're seven years old and racing each other?" asked Smith.

The other men laughed. Chase and Hunter collapsed on the ground to catch their breath.

"I wish it were that simple," Chase wheezed.

"There was an alligator not five feet away from us. Five feet. I've never been more scared in my life." Hunter looked toward the trees, as though making sure the alligator hadn't followed them.

"An alligator?" Smith asked.

"The biggest alligator I've ever seen," Chase added.

Hunter nodded. "It must have been twenty feet long."

"It was eight hundred pounds, at least," Chase agreed.

"I guess you two won't be going back there again, huh?" Smith chuckled. "It is a lake after all. The likelihood of seeing dangerous animals is pretty high."

The others laughed.

"Yeah, but not within biting distance," Hunter grumbled.

"I didn't think they had many alligators in this location," Hank said. "There's plenty down south, but no one said anything about them living around here."

"I told you they said this place was odd," Smith said. "Alligators aren't supposed to be here. Haven't you noticed all the animals acting strange? There's something off about this place. I don't think these animals are in their natural habitat."

"Well, whatever it is," Chase began, finally catching his breath, "we'll have to be more careful going forward."

Turning to the two would-be fishermen, Smith said, "Seeing as you two won't be doing any more fishing today, why don't you go upstairs and help put up the shelves and then work on the electrical wiring. We're getting close to the end so the sooner we get done with this project the sooner we get back to the lights and sounds of the city."

"Don't forget about the comforts," Hank added, his shiny baldhead was damp and reflected the sun. "I can't wait to take a real shower and sleep in a real bed without listening to you all snoring."

"I'm looking forward to a steak dinner," Hunter said.

"I think I'd like to have some fried alligator meat." Hank turned to Chase and Hunter. "Maybe one of you would like to—"

Chase and Hunter stood up and stomped into the house, leaving the others laughing.

No one noticed the little yellow frog crawling out of the forgotten sack and hopping away.

nineteen
Oh No, She Didn't

Cristobel hopped away from Sprocket Point House as the Hoppernots continued to talk. She couldn't wait to report back to her friends.

She met up with Max halfway to the lake. He looked shaken up.

"Where have you been?" Max yelled. "I've been looking all over for you. I tried to keep up with the Hoppernots after you jumped into that sack but they were too fast and they didn't head back to Sprocket Point House. I lost them and I thought I'd never see you again."

Cristobel stopped hopping. Stepping forward she put her hands out and touched Max's arm.

"Oh Max," Cristobel murmured.

Max never yelled, so Cristobel knew he was beyond upset. Even though they liked adventures, this one was more dangerous than all of their other adventures combined. When he calmed down she told him what she learned.

"They ended up at Sprocket Point House, they just went a longer, bumpier way," she said.

"What happened to your arms?" Max croaked out.

Looking down at her arm, she saw a few bruises and a couple of scratches. "Not a fun trip," she answered. "Where's Spy?"

"Spyder stayed behind in case he needed to alert anyone if we didn't come back. It all happened so fast, I don't think anyone realized you left." Max glared at her. His eyes filled with reproach for her daring.

Half of her wanted to laugh, but then she wondered if he was more upset that she jumped into the bag before he did. That put her up a notch on the adventure scorecard. Not that they were counting . . . out loud.

Feeling sorry that Max missed out on her adventure, Cristobel said, "It had to be me, Max. I'm the only one, of all the animals, who understands the Hoppernots."

"I know," he responded, his throat quivered ever so slightly.

As they approached the lake, Cristobel stopped and stared at the unusual site of Myrtle the Alligator meandering through the water, and then slowly walk onto the far shoreline. Myrtle lay on her belly and closed her eyes as she basked in the sun.

It wasn't usual for alligators to be out and about this early in the spring. They normally waited another Luna Light cycle before they drifted back to Lake Fibian, but the weather was warmer than usual, which might explain Myrtle's presence.

No one had remembered the alligators. They were not members of the Lake Fibian Collaboration, but at the lake they abided by the laws of the Agreement.

Cristobel knew she'd found their number one weapon against the Hoppernots. The only problem was getting Myrtle to help them.

While the Anura had an easy relationship with the alligators and often used the services of the Alli-Cabs to cross the lake when they didn't feel like hopping or leaping so far, but Myrtle was a different story. She was shy, temperamental, and the largest of all the alligators. She often stayed alone on the far side of the lake. The other alligators who lived at Lake Fibian left her alone, but her little brother Myron, who was the favorite of all her siblings, would be able to convince her to help.

If Myron was around. The alligators didn't always live at Lake Fibian. They were of the predator species who were prey to no one, so they tended to go from lake to lake when the whim hit them.

Once, while crossing the lake on Myron's back, he told her the Lake Fibian alligators were considered oddities at other lakes and ponds as they were the only ones who left their territories.

Cristobel smiled. "Max, I know what we need to do."

"What?" he asked.

"We're going to speak to the Collaboration Leaders. We have to convince them to ask the alligators to help us rid Lake Fibian of the Hoppernots."

"They won't like that idea," Max said. "Most of them don't like alligators like the Anura do."

Cristobel explained what she discovered back at Sprocket Point house and Max agreed.

Cristobel and Max's final hop landed them next to Spyder, but before they could tell him what happened, Foster let out four shrill, high-pitched screams causing all of the talking to immediately stop.

It was time for the Collaboration to meet now that the two Hoppernots were gone. The nervous energy around the lake crackled like a lightening storm and the animals were edgy. The larger birds of prey flew up to the higher branches where they could still listen and participate in the conversations. They would keep watch to make sure the Hoppernots did not return.

Everyone spoke at once.

"What happened?" asked a Crane. "I was almost here when I saw a couple of those Hoppernots moving as I've never seen them move before."

"They came into the water," cried a catfish. It's long whiskers brushed against the water as it kept afloat. "There were two of them. They just entered the water like they owned it and tried to kidnap us, but we outsmarted them."

A Tree Squirrel called out from a branch dangling over the water. "You should have seen them all. I've never seen the fish swim so fast." The squirrel's bushy tail swung side to side. "And then Mona faced off with those monsters and scared the fur, fins and feathers off of everyone watching. When she—"

"Quiet. Quiet everyone," Mister Webster said through the weed horn. "We can't all speak at once. I know everyone has something to contribute, but we must have order."

"The Hoppernots have become more bold and daring," Titus began. "They have brought more Mobilibeasts onto our lands, they have disrupted the quiet we are accustomed to, they have destroyed . . ." he gulped, "Destroyed Sprocket Point House and now they have tried to enter our waters and take some of our fish friends."

"We must thank Bertus for alerting us," Mona said. "If it were not for him sounding the alarm we never would have been able to get away as quickly as we did. One of us may have been taken."

A swell of water lapped up over the land as thousands of fish bobbed up and down, showing Bertus their thanks.

Bertus nodded regally.

The lake grew quiet. The Lake Fibian Collaboration was working and the leaders of each species stood together as a united front.

Cristobel opened her mouth to speak, but Spyder beat her to it.

"I know," cried Spyder. "I know one way to get wid of the Hoppewnots."

Surprised, everyone looked at him. Spyder was uncomfortable with all the eyes on him, but he knew it wasn't the time for him to feel intimidated. He had to help save his family and friends.

"When Cristobel, Max, and I were at Spwocket Point House earlier one of the Hoppewnots got sca-wed when Herman the Turkey Vulture flew at him. The Hoppewnot threw Herman's bed to the gwound and he saw it happen."

Spyder took two steps forward.

"He made the Hoppewnot scweam," he said in awe. "It was a howwi-horrible sound and not like the time the hawks or falcons flew near them. Herman was trying to attack the Hoppewnot."

"That's true," Cristobel said, "the Hoppernots were terrified of Herman, but I think . . ."

"We'll have to talk Herman into doing it again then," Miss Milly interrupted. "Although it is doubtful he will help us, the stubborn old coot."

She sniffed.

"This old coot will be more than happy to help. Even you Miss Milly," Herman called out to the group. Everyone looked up into the huge oak tree. Turning his head, Herman raised an elegant brow to Miss Milly.

Miss Milly, embarrassed at being caught talking about Herman, promptly fell to the ground, pretending to faint.

"Cristobel found out—" Max began, but was cut off.

"Let me tell you what those Hoppernots did to my home. My home I tell you," Herman voice raised. "You all come to Sprocket Point House in the summer, but I live there everyday and I keep watch too . . ."

"Funny, he never said anything when the Hoppernots *arrived*," Max mumbled.

"Get on with the story Herman. We have a war to wage and no time to listen to you babble," someone, no one would ever admit who, yelled out.

"Fine," Herman began, "Well, I was . . ."

twenty
The Fury

Herman hummed a tune by his favorite classical mixed-species band The Wilde Things as he returned to his nest after a pleasant morning soaring around the outer reaches of the lake.

It had been a lazy winter. So lazy, he stayed in his brother's redwood tree home that was beyond Lake Fibian and closer to the distant mountains for a few extra weeks instead of returning home. Herman liked his home and felt uncomfortable when he could not bed down in his own nest, but the food at his brother's place had been plentiful during the cold months and his brother was a good companion.

Feeling a little sleepy, Herman was ready for his afternoon nap. He was looking forward to dreams of warm, rotting deer flesh, but when he returned to his home he could not believe his eyes. He shook his head a few times and, knowing he had perfect vision, knew what he saw was real.

There, on the roof of Sprocket Point House was a creature he'd never seen before holding his comfortable and much missed nest. Circling in the air, Herman watched with disbelieving eyes as the evil wobble-headed creature threw his nest in the air.

Herman watched it fall to the ground, each twig and leaf he had lovingly constructed, smashed into pieces. Herman, normally an even-tempered vulture – at least that's what he thought—was furious. He threw out his wings as far as they could stretch, then flew faster and faster in a circle, gaining as much momentum as he could then he headed straight for the strange creature standing by the roof's edge.

The Hoppernot stood still, watching the bird soaring in the air. Its eyes widened as it realized it was not an eagle enjoying a glide in the sky on a beautiful day, but a vulture that looked as if it were in attack mode and heading its way.

With a yell, the Hoppernot ran across the roof and jumped through the attic window, slamming it before the angry bird could follow, but not before feeling the slight graze of the vulture's talons on the top of its head.

Clutched tightly in Herman's talons was a blue duckbill helmet.

Cristobel, Max, and Spyder were hidden in a tree, close to where the Hoppernot who'd tossed down Herman's bed had been standing. They gasped when they realized that underneath the duckbill was short dark fur that looked like moss.

When Herman was out of sight, one of the Hoppernots cracked open the window, then turned its head from side to side.

Cristobel shushed the others so she could listen to them.

"Holy Moly," the former duckbill-headed Hoppernot said. "A Turkey Vulture tried to attack me."

The Hoppernot reached up to touch its head to make sure it wasn't bleeding. "It took my favorite baseball cap. Right off my head."

"That's odd," another Hoppernot replied, scratching his chin. "They don't normally attack humans."

"Ah man, I had the last nest in my hand and threw it on the ground. It must have been his."

"That'll teach you to mess with someone else's house."

They snickered and left the room.

Max, Spyder, and Cristobel made their way down the tree. They saw a number of Hoppernots sitting in one of the rooms together. There were no Hoppernots nearby, but a few Mobilibeasts slept in the distance. They jumped onto the side of the house and hopped over to another open window.

Peering inside, they could see the Hoppernots standing around feeding. The room was filled with large objects, some with sharp edges, some rounded and other objects they'd never seen before.

"What are those things?" Spyder asked.

"No idea," Max replied.

"Shh, listen," Cristobel whispered.

They listened closely as the Hoppernot who'd destroyed Herman's home told the others what happened with the vulture.

The turtle-shelled Hoppernot asked, "Attacked, huh? I've had a weird feeling ever since we got here. It's almost as if we're being watched."

"Watched?" One of the Hoppernots, who came and went every day, drummed its fingers on its belly. The Hoppernot sat back in its seat, pushing until it was on its two back legs. "No one else lives near here and I haven't seen anyone around but us. Not even around the lake and it's filled with fish. You'd think we would have seen some fisherman out there."

"This is private property. Two hundred and twenty-six acres of private property," the turtle-shelled Hoppernot replied. "This is the kind of place people own, but they don't live in. No doubt, we'll do all this work and they'll change their minds about coming up to this place. It'll probably sit here empty like it did before. Who knows."

"Who cares," said an oak colored Hoppernot. "I'm glad me and the other people are leaving tonight and don't have to come back to this site. The wildest animal I want to encounter is a fly, thank you very much."

"Lucky you. We're stuck out here," replied the duckbill wearing Hoppernot, who had re-covered its head and now sported a bright red duckbill.

Cristobel, Max, and Spyder watched as the Hoppernots finished feeding, then stood up and left the room. The noise level began to increase and they realized the Hoppernots had returned to their destruction of Sprocket Point House.

The trio happily noticed something different this time. Each Hoppernot worked a little faster than before.

twenty-one
Decisions, Decisions

"I don't think Herman can get ww-rid of them alone," replied Spyder. He paused, realizing his tangle tongue was getting less and less pronounced. "We can surround them. Make as much noise as we can to can scare them away."

"That takessss care of you frogssss and birdssss, but what about the resssst of usssss? What can we do?" Alina asked.

"No offense Alina," Max said slowly, "but my grandfather always said the old Hoppernot was afraid of snakes because it never knew when one of you were around. Show up where they least expect it."

"Hmmm. Soundssss delicioussss. I think we can do that."

"What about us?" asked Felix, a Largemouth Bass. His head bobbed in and out of the water. "What can we do?"

"Fly out of the water as if something in there is attacking you from underneath and splash, splash, splash," Max ventured to say. He wanted to feel as if he were contributing as much as his friends. When everyone looked skeptical he said, "Or maybe you can get Myrtle to come ashore."

"Myrtle?" Mantu asked. He flew down to the ground and stood next to Foster. "Is she back already?"

"Myrtle?" Spyder asked, surprised. "She's uhh, she's . . ."

"Too darn shy," a voice from above yelled.

Many heads nodded in agreement.

"True, but the Hoppernots are terrified of her. Go ahead Cristobel. Tell them," Max nudged her in front of the group.

"I've been trying to," she mumbled.

Hoping she wouldn't get in trouble, Cristobel told them what they saw at the lake and what she'd overheard at Sprocket Point House. While many of the

Anura Elders and Collaboration Leaders glared at her, no one could argue with her information, which might be the key to getting rid of the Hoppernots.

Cristobel ended, "Myrtle is the largest land-water dweller at the lake, but we have to convince her to help us. The Alligators are not part of the Collaborations. She may say no."

"But if we get Myrtle to help us, then the other alligators will help too," Max added.

"I'll go talk to Myrtle," Felix said, "I saw her slip into the water. He disappeared beneath the water.

"These are all wonderful ideas," said Mister Webster, coming forward and standing next to Cristobel, Max, and Spyder. "This may be the best . . . the only way to be rid of the Hoppernots."

"I must say I am proud of these young ones," Mantu said, then raised his voice. "We should all be proud of them."

Titus hopped over and laid his webbed hands on top of Max and Spyder's heads.

Mister Webster beamed down at Cristobel, then over at Max and Spyder. "Who would have thought these three rascals would go beyond everyone's expectation," he mused.

"I think," Foster began, "it's time to send Cristobel, Spyder, and Max to where the other leaplings are hiding. The next part of this battle will be dangerous."

"I disagree, Foster," Mantu replied. "These little frogs have done more for us than anyone else. They've been strong and courageous. They deserve to be part of this."

Mister Webster stepped forward. "I agree with Foster. None of the other leaplings or youngsters of any other species have helped in this war. We should not make any exceptions."

"Don't you mean any more exceptionssss, Mister Webster?" Alina asked. "I agree with Mantu. *The Three* are sssstronger than they look."

Alina turned her head toward Cristobel, Max, and Spyder, and then lowered her head in acknowledgement.

The Elders brought *The Three*'s families forward.

Standing together, Max's tiny green grandmother and Spyder's stout red and blue mother sat back on their hind legs. Both crossed their vibrantly colored arms and announced in unison, "Both our families have spoken and we agree with Foster and Mister Fowler."

Miss Milly stepped closer to Julius, Cristobel's father. She grabbed his arm and leveled a fierce gaze at the other Elders. Before Julius could open his mouth, Miss Milly said, "We agreed with Mantu."

"That'ssss ssssurprising," Alina hissed.

Cristobel's mother was silent. Notty stood with her back to the arguing members of the Collaboration and watched her daughter and her two best friends huddled together.

Before she could voice her vote, *The Three* stepped forward holding hands.

"We've shown how dedicated we are and we've listened and followed directions," Cristobel said.

"We haven't gotten into trouble and we won't," Max added.

Notty stepped up to the trio and kissed each on top of their heads, then faced the gathering. "They even became leaders when the Collaboration Leaders couldn't lead themselves."

Notty looked around, staring unblinking at the familiar faces. "All along I have wondered if they would take the threats seriously. Would they cause trouble? Would they get hurt? Like you, I don't want anything to happen to these little ones, but they must continue what they started."

More grumbles erupted, until Notty stepped into the circle of the crowd and asked what she already knew the answer to, "Is there anyone, any species, who understands the Hoppernots?"

Species after species said no. Again.

"No, Mama," Cristobel answered. "I'm still the only one."

"Then let them join," Notty said, her voice quiet, but firm. "They can help. We need Cristobel and she needs Max and Spyder. I believe in them and so should you."

Notty gazed at the other family members, then at the Collaboration Leaders. "You know I'm right. You may not want to admit it, but you know I am right."

"When shall we begin?" asked Benjamin, a Snowy Owl. He was standing straighter than usual, with a gleam in his eye. He was ready to battle. Benjamin came from a long line of hunters.

"We'll need a few more days," Titus suggested.

"But first we have to get the alligators to agree and make sure they are ready," Cristobel said.

"It will take that long to get them close to Spwocket Point House," Spyder added. "You know how slow they walk."

"In a few days then," Mister Webster said. He took a deep breath and expanded his chest.

He opened his mouth to begin giving orders, but was interrupted by an excited red frog, followed by two orange frogs, leaping from tree to tree.

"He's awake! He's awake!" Doctor Tom cried. "Mister Fowler finally opened his eyes and do you know what he said?"

Before anyone respond, Doctor Tom said, "He asked for a cup of Chipmunk Delight and a fly-pop." Doctor Tom laughed, although he laughed alone. "He's going to be okay."

After a moment of stunned silence, everyone cheered.

"Food is always the best medicine," Spyder said.

"That is wonderful news," said Mister Webster. Happy to hear his friend would be all right, he slumped against a tree. "Being Mayor is not as fun as you'd think."

"What perfect timing," Titus exclaimed. "We needed this news to boost our spirits!"

Mantu and Fowler stood tall behind the Elder frogs and Alina hung down from the tree above them.

Mantu raised his voice. "We must be ready to chase the Hoppernots away from Lake Fibian."

"Spread the word and recruit as many of the new arrivals as you can," Max added.

The animals began to leave. Foster leaped into the air and then, without warning, he dropped back down to the ground and stepped closer to Mantu.

Everyone stopped moving, wondering what new argument would start between these two.

Foster looked Mantu in the eye for a full five seconds and, to the surprise of every animal present, slowly inclined his head. "If one suffers, we all suffer.

So let's spread out and rest for the night. In unity we will work together and in unity we will succeed."

"This will be the biggest battle of our lives," Mantu added. "Let's be ready for them."

Cheers broke out all around the lake. The crowd broke apart. Members of each species went their separate ways to plan on how best to use their most fierce fighting skills and then, most importantly, to be with their families maybe for the last time.

When the Collaboration Leaders, along with *The Three,* were the only animals standing around, Titus began the most difficult conversation.

"We need a plan in place for casualties. Each species must know where to go and what to do if there are injuries," Titus said.

"Or deaths," Spyder added.

twenty-two
A Secret Revealed

Later, as Cristobel, Max, and Spyder hopped toward their homes with Mantu flying above them as guard, Cristobel thought about her special skill.

"I don't know if this skill is new or if I've always had it," Cristobel said.

"You'll never know if you've always had it 'cause you've never seen a Hoppewnot before," Spyder replied.

"That's true," she sighed. "I thought there'd be others who understood their language, at least someone else from the Polka-Dot Tree frogs. It doesn't make sense."

"Hoppernots don't make sense," said Max, "so since they exist, it only makes sense that you understand them."

"That doesn't make any sense, Max," Cristobel said. She closed her eyes and concentrated.

"What is it, Cristobel?" Mantu asked.

"This'll sound crazy, but I think it must be something I did," she replied, then said softly, "Or something I ate."

"What did you say?"

I think I know why or . . ." Cristobel began, "I think I know how I can understand the Hoppernots."

Spyder and Max stopped hopping. Mantu, hearing her, flew down to the ground. They looked at her expectedly and, in horror, admiration, and a teeny bit of envy as Cristobel said, "Last year, right after the leaves turned color, but before they fell, I ate a berry from the Prickle Berry bush."

"The fowbidden Pwickle Bewwy bush?" Spyder asked.

Max's eyes bulged and he sat back on his hind legs, placing his arms on the ground. "Why didn't you tell us, Cristobel? I thought we didn't keep secrets from each other."

"I-I couldn't, Max. It was an accident."

Max and even Spyder looked skeptical.

"I found the berries when I was snacking on mosquitoes by Beaver Brook." She looked over at Spyder, knowing he would understand.

"It was a big fat mosquito. It landed on a leaf or what I thought was a leaf. What I couldn't see from the side I approached was that the mosquito was on a Prickle Berry that fell on the ground. The leaf hid the berry from view and it was too late."

Cristobel looked over at Max and Mantu. "Once I released my tongue and caught the mosquito and the berry I couldn't stop. I had to eat them both. I would have told you, but I was scared."

Spyder leaned toward Cristobel and whisper in awe, "The Pwickle Bewwy is the most dangerous bewwy there is."

"I know, but when I didn't get sick or die, I thought I shouldn't mention it to anyone, and then the Hoppernots arrived . . ."

She trailed off, dropping her eyes to the ground.

Spyder hopped over and laid a hand over hers.

"It's okay Crithobel. I pwobably would have eaten it too."

"Well, I'm glad you didn't get sick," Max said grudgingly. "Or die."

Max stepped closer and took her other hand.

"Cristobel, why do you think the Prickle Berry gave you your ability?" Mantu asked.

"It's the only thing I ever did differently. I never would've eaten a forbidden berry if I knew it was there. Never."

"According to the Croaklore, you should have died on the spot or became so ill you wish you had," Max said.

"I am familiar with that Croaklore," Mantu said, surprising the trio. "There were a number of serious illnesses among the Anura and a few of the Bird species many, many summers ago."

"It's what my family believes Cousin Tess ate that caused her to loose her froggy mind," Cristobel said.

"Weally?" Spyder asked. "I never heard that."

"You wouldn't have. It's not something spoken of outside my family and only a few of the Elders know about it." Cristobel slumped down. "All that time, I thought I was losing my mind too, but I felt – and still feel – fine. Well, other than understanding Hoppernots."

"Hmm," Mantu murmured. "Just because you ate a forbidden fruit, doesn't mean that it's the reason for your ability."

"Maybe we should tell the Collaboration Leaders," Cristobel suggested.

Mantu leaned over to look eye-to-eye with the leaplings.

"No. We don't know if it was the berry, so let's we keep this to ourselves," Mantu said. "Not only will you be in serious trouble with the Anura, but the Prickle Berry bush is forbidden—to all of the animals—for a reason. You'll be punished and it will distract everyone from our mission."

"How did you know I'd eaten it?" Cristobel asked. "You mentioned it before."

"I saw you do it, but there wasn't much I could do at the time. I was about to leave for the Deep Sleep and needed to get my murder coordinated. I watched after you while I was here to make sure you were all right. I could see how terrified you were, Cristobel, but since you never got sick or died I kept your secret. Besides, I too have had a purple prickle berry, and I'm as alive and as sane as you are. I don't think it's the berry making you understand the Hoppernots, because I do not and I never did."

Max opened his mouth to ask how and why, but Mantu cut him off.

"It's old news, Max and I'll never tell."

Mantu leaped in the air and spread his black wings. "Let's get you home now."

The four of them now shared a secret they could never tell.

They resumed hopping toward home again, each one of them thoughtful. But Spyder, with his insatiable one-track mind broke the silence.

"Crithobel, what does the Prickle Berry taste like?"

twenty-three
The Stance

The morning was gloriously cool. The sky was cloudless. The sun's warmth felt like a hug from a grandparent. It was the kind of day you splashed in a pool or napped in the sun.

The animals of Lake Fibian did not notice. Even though no one got much sleep during the night, there was an air of excitement tinged with anxiety.

Mister Webster, Titus, and Miss Milly sat up high in a tree with Max, Spyder, and Cristobel. Each shook or croaked quietly while they waited for the Hoppernots to appear.

"They're not here yet," Miss Milly whispered.

"Be patient Miss Milly," Titus said, patting her hand.

Mister Webster and Spyder stood on the branch above watching out for any sign of the Hoppernots' return. Spyder's leg twitched like crazy.

Max and Cristobel sat on a branch below the others and looked around. They watched as their friends and family took their places in trees and around the house.

"Let's go through the check list," Titus suggested.

"The squirrels are ready to go," Max announced.

Squirrels hung from trees upside down and right-side up. The lower tree trunks looked like furry leggings. Webbed sacks made by the spiders' quick legs, filled with acorns ready to throw, hung down each squirrel's back.

"The turtles and tortoises are in place," Cristobel said.

Turtles and tortoises were spaced out across the ground hiding behind rocks or bushes. They were tucked inside their shells and ready to defend when the time came.

"The birds are on the wooftop and ww-railings of the house," Spyder called out.

The birds' sharp, watchful eyes darted around looking for disturbances. They called a few quiet *coos* and *caws* back and forth, letting the others know they were ready and waiting. A few of the birds stepped back, ready to take cover once the Hoppernots were spotted. They didn't want to blow their cover before they were ready.

The Three continued to check each animal's position, while Titus marked them off his scroll.

Dozens of eagles and ospreys hid high in the trees, ready to take flight and give chase.

The Gliding Tree Frogs were ready to dive. They stood in the shadow of the birds, sitting on low hanging branches watching and waiting.

The Burrowing Owls were silent and underground. The holes in the earth were covered with enough moss to conceal them, but allow them see.

Within the hour, each animal species of Lake Fibian surrounded Sprocket Point House—those of the land and air. All of them waited.

At the lake, the fish bobbed up and down in the water creating a slight wave. No one swam or jumped. They kept their eyes to the sky waiting for their signal from Mantu.

Around the lake, silence reigned. Nerves were stretched tighter than a coiled snake ready to strike. Each little sound caused premature jumping, chirping, burping, and a few wet spots to appear.

Sooner than most were ready, the overwhelming quiet was broken by Bertus' warning call and then they heard the sounds of the Mobilibeasts stalking towards them in the woods.

All eyes were on the Mobilibeasts as they slowed down to a crawl, and then stopped in front of the house. Their growls turned to purrs and then silence as the Hoppernots, one by one, exited the ears of the Mobilibeasts.

The Hoppernots walked to the last project they had been working on the day before.

"This place is a mess. We need to clean up," the turtle-shelled Hoppernot, called out.

The animals watched as some of the Hoppernots moved as if weighed down by stones, dragging their strange bodies up the porch or across the grass, while other Hoppernots rushed through, picking up odd objects and throwing them into square containers or into the rear ends of the quiet Mobilibeasts.

Cristobel softly interpreted what the Hoppernots were saying.

"This old house is perfect," the turtle-shelled Hoppernot said. "Or as close to perfect as any one hundred and twenty year old house can be way out in the woods with no people in sight."

"I sure wish the other people had stuck around longer and helped us clean up," the porcupine head, groused.

Cristobel gasped, "The Pee-ple are gone. All we have to do is worry about the Hoppernots."

"What?" Titus yelped.

Cristobel shushed him and pointed back to the Hoppernots below.

"They were happy to see the back of this place," the duckbill-headed Hoppernot said. "The last few days have been real strange. The woods are either too quiet or filled with so much chirpin', squawkin' and squealin' you have to cover your ears to think."

The Hoppernots walked toward Sprocket Point House. None of them spoke, but all of a sudden they looked around, eyes wide.

"It's real quiet, don't you think?" the turtle-shelled Hoppernot murmured. "Quieter than it's been the whole time we've been here. I don't even hear the leaves rustling."

The turtle-shelled Hoppernot stood on the top step of the porch and listened to the silence of the woods. "Yeah. Too quiet," it said, looking around.

"Woods are never this kind of quiet unless something's wrong."

"I feel uneasy," the duckbill-headed Hoppernot said.

"I've got a kind of chill," the turtle-shelled Hoppernot replied. They looked at each other, eyes wide.

"Let's get inside."

The only sounds in the woods were the noises coming through the open front door. Every animal stared at the house, watching the Hoppernots enter and exit.

They were taking things out of the house. A few of the Hoppernots struggled down the stairs as they carried large square boxes.

"They get rid of my pillow, toss it out like it's a mud patty, but carry those ugly things out like they're treasures," Miss Milly mumbled. Cristobel shushed her.

Miss Milly was about to remind her that she was the Elder when Titus gave her a stern look. She closed her mouth, but would remember to speak to Cristobel about her rudeness later.

The animals were waiting for the perfect moment when all the Hoppernots were out of the house and standing together.

Doctor Tom was waiting in a safe zone with the doctors of the other species. They set up a makeshift clinic with all of the medicines and equipment each species would need in case there were any injuries.

The night before Doctor Tom told the Collaboration Leaders that if one Hoppernot were scared, they would all be scared and their fear would grow. Most were doubtful and wanted to run them out one by one, but he pointed out that since the entire population of Lake Fibian would be surrounding them, fear would be the first reaction and, with luck, flight would be the second. The other doctors agreed.

So, they prepared to wait.

It was time.

Most of the Hoppernots filed out of the house. They looked around, but kept silent. The animals could see some of them twitch, while others breaths stopped in their throats. There was a sense of satisfaction as all the animals noticed the Hoppernots eyes widened.

On the ground, in the trees, even on the roof of the house were hundreds and hundreds of animals silently staring at them, not moving even by a feather flutter.

The owls stayed in the shade of the trees and hooted. The Hoppernots, hearing the eerie night sounds cutting through the sunny daylight hours, shifted uneasily.

Foster's sharp eyes saw the tiny hairs on the Hoppernots necks stand in fear. He chuckled at the sight.

Owls were night creatures and normally asleep during the day. Hearing them while the sun was up was not a good omen and while the Hoppernots could hear the owls, they could not see them. They were in the trees, high and hidden behind leafy branches and deep burrows.

Smith was the last Hoppernot to depart the house. A tinkling sound rang out as the locked clicked close. Turning around, Smith bumped into Hunter.

"What's going on? Why are you standing around like this?" Smith was about to push through the motionless men when he noticed the animals surrounding them. It took a few seconds before the level of quiet in the woods had risen to a deafening silence.

Something was wrong. Very wrong.

twenty-four
Retreat of the Beasts

Without warning, the Hoppernots heard the loudest, longest *croaks* of their lives, and then the air was filled with flying objects and animals.

"Aim. Fire," Max yelled.

Squirrels threw shells.

Blue jays and swallows hurled twigs and leaves.

Gray squirrels tossed their precious nuts.

Cristobel hopped up several branches and called out, "Yell, scream, make noise!" She joined in with the other animals croaking until she was dizzy.

More sounds erupted when the first acorn hit one of the Hoppernots in the face. Screeching, grunts, caws, and loud burping sounds from the frogs reverberated on the air.

Snakes slithered toward the steps, hissing and spitting their way towards the Hoppernots who were standing paralyzed in fear.

Spyder inhaled as much air as his lungs could take, then yelled, “Fly, dive, soar.”

Eagles, sparrows, herons, egrets, spoonbills, and hawks flew above Sprocket Point House in a circular pattern. They were led by a gleeful Herman. There were so many of them they shaded the house from the sun.

“This is gw-great,” Spyder exclaimed.

“Look! Look at Max,” Cristobel said.

“Go Max, go,” Spyder encouraged.

“Be careful, Max.”

The turtle-shelled Hoppernot ducked as Max flew at his head. Max was an amazing sight to see as everyone would later recall. He did a spin in the air to redirect himself as the Hoppernot ducked. His webbed hands grabbed the Hoppernot’s ear and held on tight.

The Hoppernot lifted its hand, swiping at its ear. Max went flying through the air, but managed to land on the base of a tree and was cushioned by the bushy tail of a squirrel.

The porcupine-headed Hoppernot looked up and let out a yell when a red-winged black bird made a dive towards it, but it shut its mouth as smelly gray matter covered its head and face.

The red wing screeched out a jubilant *chak, chak, chak* call in satisfaction of seeing its thick pungent droppings cover the Hoppernots mouth. The Hoppernot jumped up and down, spitting and gagging.

"Your turn red squirrels," Cristobel called out.

The red squirrels, the most feared of the squirrel clan, performed an impressive show. A peevish group – their frenzied race around and around the tree trunks seemed to unsettle the Hoppernots. The red squirrels were upset the Hoppernots had dug up the large oak tree—their main storage area—and destroyed the acorns, mushrooms, and the cones they had meticulously stowed away.

Spyder picked up his twitching leg and began rapidly striking the tree trunk, giving the rabbits their cue.

Some of the rabbit warrens jumped high in the air, while others thumped their paws on the ground. *Thump-thump-thump-thump.*

Cristobel, Max, and Spyder leaped down to a lower branch, opened their throats and let out the Anura warning call.

As one, the frog nation raised their voices. They *croaked, chirped, clacked, buzzed, whistled, grunted* and made all the noises each species was known for.

The owls joined in. Their eerie *hoohoo-hoohoo*, sounded more like a lulling invitation than a threat.

Hundreds of gray squirrels ran up and down the trees they called home, jumping from tree to tree screeching as loud as their little lungs allowed.

Spyder and Cristobel leaped down, then jumped from tree to tree until they sat on the tip of a branch in a tree farther from the house. Their job was to direct the alligators. When they heard Benjamin's call alerting them of the alligators arrival they leaped to the ground to take up their position on Myrtle's back.

Max was waiting for them to give him the signal and the all clear *croak*. When Spyder raised his arm and wiggled his fingers, Max grinned and made his way over. He plopped down next to his friends.

It had not been easy to convince Myrtle. When her brother Myron spoke to her she told him no. For days he followed her around the lake and tried to convince her to help the other animals, but she stubbornly refused to listen to him.

They other animals, while disappointed, were not surprised by her refusal, but Cristobel, Max, and Spyder, after talking it over with the Collaboration Leaders, tried one last time and much to the surprise of everyone, it was Spyder who convinced her to help them.

They found Myrtle hidden in a low copse of trees on the far side of the lake. She was alone as she usually was. She had just come out of the water when they approached her. Droplets clung to her skin and the tips of her scales as she lay stretched out in the grass, asleep in the sun.

Spyder, Max, and Cristobel clung to the side of a tree watching her. It had been a long journey to find her as they hopped and leaped the entire way, leaving the Collaboration Leaders waiting for them. They were exhausted.

"Let's go over there," Max said. He pointed to a boulder two feet from Myrtle's head. They hopped to the boulder and slowly made their way up the side until they reached the top. They stood quietly and looked down at Myrtle's long rounded snout and closed eyelids.

Cristobel called out, "Myrtle. Myrtle, wake up." Her voice was so soft the light wind caught her words and whipped them away.

Max scrunched his face and looked at Cristobel. “That’s not the way to wake up an alligator.”

Placing his fingers next to his mouth, he pulled air into his throat and sent out a piercing *croak*. When Myrtle’s tail twitched he yelled, “Hey Myrtle, wake up. We need to talk to you. It’s important stuff.”

Myrtle’s eyelids slid open. She slowly lifted her head, then faster than lightening, moved her body to the left and the right. She dropped her jaw, baring her sharp teeth as her eyes scanned the area looking an intruder. She walked in a full circle, eyes wide and watchful.

Myrtle stood alert for a few moments, listening carefully, then lowered her body back to the ground. She closed her eyes.

“Myrtle, don’t go back to sleep. We’re up here.”

Max waved his green arms and then nudged Spyder who also raised his bright red arms and waved them in a short jerky motion.

Lifting her eyes she spied three tiny creatures. Snapping her jaw shut, she growled, “Who are you? I can’t see you way up there.”

“It’s Cristobel, Max, and Spyder,” Cristobel called out. “We’re from the Anura.”

“Oh. You three. I know who you are,” she grumbled. “You’re the three bad frogs who always get into trouble?”

Myrtle's soft voice was at odds with the size of her body.

"We are not bad," Max said. He hopped down the side of the boulder. Spying a smaller rock below, he pushed off with his hind legs and landed on a smaller rock in front of Myrtle. They stood eye-to-eye.

In a voice that trembled, Max said, "We're not bad. We're just a little bit naughty."

With a soft *thwack* Spyder and Cristobel landed next to Max, making him jump. Spyder reached out and clasped Cristobel's hand.

Myrtle was the largest and scariest of all the alligators. Most of the alligators were easy to get along with and many were used as Alli-Cabs who shuttled some of the smaller creatures around the lake, but not Myrtle.

Myrtle kept to herself and for years, the animals of Lake Fibian whispered that she was mean and vicious. There were stories of her chasing after other animals or swinging her large heavy tail around to try and hit anyone who got to close to her, but her brother Myron set everyone straight: Myrtle was not mean, she was just shy and cautious.

When she was young, she was teased so much about her oversized body that she retreated into her self. Being the largest alligator in the pod might seem like a good thing, but not when you are ruthlessly teased about something you have no control over. As an adult alligator, Myrtle was happy to be alone or with Myron, her favorite brother.

"Bad or naughty," Myrtle grumbled, "You three are always in trouble and now you're trying to bring trouble to me. No, thank you."

Turning her body around, she began to walk toward the water.

"But we need your help," Cristobel called out. "Lake Fibian – our home – has been invaded by Hoppernots. We need to make them leave. We need you."

Myrtle avoided looking at the trio when she said, "I have other homes. Besides this has nothing to do with me."

"Of course it does," Max insisted. "You live here sometimes, and so does your family and the other alligators. We need you. We need to work together."

"Why should I help you? I'm not a part of the Lake Fibian Collaboration. I don't feel comfortable around so many animals and I'm not comfortable around the other alligators, but you want me to come face to face with these Hopping creatures."

"They're called Hoppernots and they are destroying our homes . . . *your* home," Max said.

"Myrtle," Cristobel said gently, "you are our only hope. They're afraid of you."

"How do you know?" Myrtle asked. "I've never seen a Hoppernot before."

"They've seen you and when they did they wan away," Spyder said. Although he was afraid of her, he hopped closer. "All of the animals are working together to get www-rid of them, Myrtle. Please help us."

"I don't know," Myrtle said. She lowered her large body to the ground and closed her eyes. "I would have to be around everyone and I don't know anything about Hoppernots."

"I'm sca-wed too, Myrtle," Spyder said. "But I'm more sca-wed of someone losing their life."

Myrtle sighed. "I really don't want to."

"You and me are alike, Myrtle. I weally don't want to either. I don't like being awound all the other species at once. They're big, I'm small and I'm always afwaid they'll tell me I have leave my two best fww-friends to hide with the others because I don't have a lot of courage, I eat too much and I don't talk like everyone else. This is my way to prove that I am brr-brave even with my tangled tongue and big belly."

Myrtle lowered her eyes and tapped her teeth together.

What if I stay with you?" Spyder asked.

"What?" Cristobel and Max asked.

Spyder flipped around to face his friends. "She's sca-wed. I'm sca-wed. I'll be less sca-wed if I'm with her and she won't have to feel alone. It's the perfect plan."

Cristobel was about to argue.

As he said, Spyder was not the most courageous of frogs and he was terrified of Myrtle, but as Cristobel opened her mouth to speak, she noticed the alligator staring at the little red and blue frog. Myrtle's mouth hung open slightly. It looked as if she was smiling, if alligators smiled.

Myrtle said, "A tangle tongued frog, huh?"

"Yup," Spyder replied, "and I'm pwoud of it, too."

Myrtle's eyes took in the three little frogs standing before her looking scared but resolute.

"Okay," she agreed. "If you stay with me during the battle, I'll go. I'll help you with the Hoppernots."

The trio croaked in glee.

Spyder breathed deep and sent out the "mission accomplished" call to the rest of the animals.

Watching the scene below, the leaders of the Collaboration were pleased they were able to convince the alligators to help them. They were proud of Myrtle. All of Lake Fibian was relying on her to be as fierce as she could be.

"Holy Cow," the turtle-shelled Hoppernot shouted, breaking the silence. "Is that the . . ." he gasped.

Myrtle stood in front of the Hoppernots with Cristobel, Max, and Spyder crouched low on her back each holding on to a spike. She was glaring at the Hoppernots as though she wanted to eat them. The animals closest to the house were impressed by her ferocity.

Mantu stood next to her like a bad omen stalking the Hoppernots. His murder flew down and surrounded them as they stacked forward.

The Hoppernots hovering near the steps gaped at the approaching alligators, crows, and hissing snakes that were fast approaching their legs.

"No, not the cars. I hope they don't get too close to the cars," a Hoppernots said from the back. "We'll never get out of here."

At the sounds of their voices, Myrtle stalked toward the Hoppernots now standing huddled together. She opened her mouth as wide as she could and snapped her jaw shut.

The sound of Myrtle's strong jaw clicking close seemed to startle the Hoppernots out of their fright.

They ran.

Tobias stood up and the other turtles followed. They tripped the Hoppernots as they ran toward the Mobilibeasts.

Cristobel, Max, and Spyder watched with growing anxiety as the Hoppernots neared the Mobilibeasts and then jumped over their brave snake friends.

Fearless Alina jumped on top of the big black Mobilibeast, but one of the Hoppernots grabbed her by her tail and hurled her into the air. She hissed as she flew and landed on a tree branch, nearly knocking Miss Milly over.

Angry birds pecked the Hoppernots heads, shoulders, backs, and arms as they pushed each other into the ears of the Mobilibeasts.

"What do you think they'll do?" asked Cristobel, leaping off Myrtle's back and onto a stump.

"I don't know, but if the Mobilibeasts attack, Miss Milly will alert whoever is in the way," replied Max, following her.

Spyder stayed where he was. He was quiet and his eyes were unusually large. He watched as two Hoppernots race towards the sleeping chamber.

"What are they doing?" he asked.

Mantu, Max, and Cristobel looked over toward the box and heard a loud, angry roar.

"It's a Mobilibeast!" *The Three* exclaimed together.

The box began moving, slowly at first, snaking in and out of the trees and aiming at animals too shocked to move quickly.

The turtles were in trouble. There were three large tortoises trying to move out of the way, but the weight of their shells and their small stumpy legs would go no faster than normal.

"Foster," Cristobel cried, "help."

Before the Mobilibeast began its attack, Foster and two other eagles swooped down from the sky, grabbed hold of the tortoises' shells and flew them to safety. The Mobilibeast stopped suddenly and Cristobel heard a Hoppernot yell, "Are you kidding me?"

Then the Mobilibeast let out one loud roar and bounded down the newly made pathway and away from Sprocket Point House.

The Mobilibeast closest to Titus and Mister Webster roared when the Hoppernots jumped into its ears. The sound of the other Mobilibeasts' furious growls vibrated throughout the clearing, scaring everyone.

The black Mobilibeast lunged forward, but stopped when large black wings blocked the vision of the Hoppernot in the driver's seat. Blooblaq, the ferocious Black Vulture no one thought to ask to help, suddenly appeared, swooped down and hovered close to the glass.

Blooblaq and the Hoppernot stared at each other for a solid minute. The Hoppernot began to shake and Blooblaq screeched before he flew away. The message was given and received: *Don't come back.*

The big black Mobilibeast rushed toward Myrtle. She was scared, but she stood her ground and did not move. She could feel Spyder shaking on her back.

The other two Mobilibeasts followed, chasing after squirrels and forcing the birds that flew down to the ground to fly up high and out of the way.

Tobias didn't move. Not because he was brave, but because he was so scared he could not get his body to listen to his brain or to the others around him who were screeching for him to retreat. Dropping to lie flat down on his shell, he tucked his arms, legs and head inside. He was shaking like a leaf in the breeze.

The Mobilibeasts were near their prey, but at the last minute the black, the red, and the blue monsters swerved around, narrowly missing Myrtle and Spyder, and the other animals still on the ground.

Just as the blue Mobilibeast passed Tobias, it used its round back leg to knock into his shell spinning him in dizzying circles.

The Mobilibeast began running faster and faster, leaving dust and quiet behind them.

As they drove off, Chase looked toward the lake and through the trees he saw hundreds, maybe thousands of fish leaping out of the water. He nudged Hunter, who poked the man sitting next to him, and with a nod toward the lake, indicated the animal madness was not only on land and in the air.

"You couldn't pay me to go back there," Hunter yelled, wrinkling his nose as the scent of his friend, whom the red-winged black bird targeted, reached his nose.

"Nope, not even for a billion bucks and all the frog legs I can eat," Chase agreed. His loud voice carried on the air. "Those Herpetologists must be insane to want to move out here."

No one made a sound for twenty minutes. Thirty. After a full hour had passed the animals looked around at each other with dawning realization.

They'd won.

They had succeeded in driving the Hoppernots from Sprocket Point House and away from Lake Fibian. All of them. Not a single Hoppernot or Mobilibeast was in sight.

"I have a feeling we won't be seeing them ever again," Miss Milly cried and fainted into Doctor Tom's arms.

When Doctor Tom learned the Hoppernots had run away from Sprocket Point House like a bunch of scared hedgehogs, he left the Burrow and joined the rest of his friends. He made it a point to stand next to Miss Milly; she hadn't fainted in a while and was due for a good long one.

High above, a fast moving object created a shadow on the ground. Every head looked up.

"They're gone," said Mister Fowler who was sitting on Foster's back. Since he hadn't fully healed from the Mobilibeasts' attack, the Anura leaders, approved by Doctor Tom, decided Mister Fowler shouldn't be involved since he was the first casualty of the Hoppernot invasion, but Mister Fowler insisted on doing his part since he missed so much of the adventure.

Mister Fowler and Foster had flown to the edge of the woods and sat near the one road that led in and out of Lake Fibian to keep watch.

"Herman, Blooblaq, and Mantu are going to follow them and make sure they don't return," Foster chuckled. "I think they're going to like convincing them to stay away. I may even join them."

Pushing off, he spread his wings and followed. A grin split his face at the idea of a chase.

"What's a Herpetologist?" Cristobel asked, but her question was drowned out by the noise of the crowd. It was forgotten in the excitement and the crush of arms as Notty and Julius hugged and kissed her then pulled Max and Spyder into their embrace until their own families pushed through the crowds and joined in.

"They're gone!" everyone yelled, their voices growing louder to make sure everyone in and around the lake heard the news.

"They're gone!" Max shouted.

"Gone?" Cristobel asked. "For good?"

"Of course, for good, Crithobel." Spyder said and then hugged her. "We scared them away."

"I don't know what you all did," Mister Fowler said, "but they ran out of here so fast I barely saw them through the dust. I don't think they'll ever step foot on our land again."

Mister Fowler laughed. His belly jiggled so much he fell off of Foster. Luckily he fell on top of rabbit who happily broke his fall.

"This calls for a celebration," said Mister Webster raising his hand, he pointed two fingers in the air. "One, two, three . . ."

Once upon a time
On the Lake of Fibian
Lake Fibian...

Vocabulary

(alphabetical order)

Alli-Cab – Alligators who provide rides across the lake to smaller animals and birds.

Anura – the name of the entire frog species.

Barrier Lake – A forbidden place where the rules of living does not exist.

Basin of Taynt – A forbidden place.

Chipmunk Delight – A special brew made from wild plums, worms, fly legs, and blueberries.

Code Hoppernot – The highest warning signal of the Concord Pact that is shared between all animals living around Lake Fibian and apart of the Lake Fibian Collaboration.

Concord Pact – Common warning call every animal species use to alert each other to danger.

Croaklore – Mostly true stories and cautionary tales of the history and happenings of Lake Fibian, told by the frog Elders.

Deep Sleep - The long hibernation during the cold winter months.

Frog Salsa – A hopping, bouncing, leaping dance.

Hoppernot – A human, either male of female.

Hopping Shoot – A walking (or hopping) cane.

Lake Fibian – The lakefront where the Anura and other animals live harmoniously…or according the Concord Pact.

Lake Fibian Collaboration – A committee of the highest-ranking members of every animal species.

Leaferchief – A frog's version of a handkerchief.

Leapling – A young frog who has already lost its tail.

Luna Light Night – The Anura's monthly celebration on the night of the full moon.

Mobilibeast – A car or truck.

Napp-in – Not quite a hibernation but close. These animals do not sleep the entire winter season, but can and do move around and forage for food throughout the cold months.
Nip-Snapper – A biter.

Pee-Ple – Human beings.

Prickle Berry – A dangerous fruit all of the animals are forbidden to eat.

Sib-leapling – An only frog child.

Spadefoots – The band made up of frogs who play the Lake Fibian Anthem on Luna Light Night.

Sprocket Point House – The summer vacation house used by most of the animals around Lake Fibian. Formerly, the original Hoppernot's home.

Stinkweed – A stinky scented plant that revives patients.

Tadnap – The frog's version of kidnap.

Tangle Tongue – Spyder's speech pattern.

The Burrow – The hospital for the Anura.

The Three – The name the Anura call Max, Cristobel, and Spyder.

Weedhorn – A hollow plant shoot used to project the voice.

Acknowledgements

Deep appreciation goes to my parents, Meva and Trevor Blake, who taught me about love, focus, taking chances, and who instilled in me a strong work ethic and belief in myself.

To my sisters and brother, Shirley, Maureen, and Vivion who helped me become the person I am today. Thank you all for being awesome.

A heartfelt thanks to my wonderful NH critique group. Special recognition goes to the Poet (Matthew Forrest), the Non-Fiction Writer and Animal Lover (Miranda Levin), and the Historical Adventurer (Stephen Capraro) for the many, many months of reading, reviewing, and providing invaluable insights.

To Jordan Rosenfeld, who not only edited The Hoppernots but also helped me see how much better the story could be with new eyes.

To Jet Kimchrea, illustrator extraordinaire, watching your own evolution as an artist inspired me to do and be bigger. Thanks for the amazing collaboration.

To Matthew Chan who enthusiastically read my book and asked for Book Two already. Thanks for being a true reader.

To Kerry Kriger, PhD, founder of Save the Frogs, many thanks for creating an amazing organization that teaches the world the importance of amphibians, the care of the earth, and why saving frogs are so important to human life.

To my family of friends who supported and cheered me on, you kept my spirits up even when I wondered where my writing would take me. You all rock!

To my awesome husband Joe, thank you so much for believing in and supporting me every single day. You've made this writing to author journey that much more exquisite.

Deborah Blake Dempsey is a New Yorker by birth, a Floridian by the number of years raised there, and a New Englander by choice. She loves good books, belly laughs, fabulous shoes, and travel. She has a twisted sense of humor and truly believes laughter is the elixir of life. Deborah currently lives in New Hampshire with her husband Joe. ***The Hoppernots*** is her debut novel.

CPSIA information can be obtained at www.ICGtesting.com
Printed in the USA
LVOW07s0049050915

452957LV00001B/43/P